IN D

By Sarah

Villas, fast cars and champagne is everything Tate could wish for but hidden behind the luxury is a dark and seedy world, fraught with danger. Bill is everything she desires, and despite his lack of commitment and questionable career he has Tate's heart.

Bill is clinging to a life he has grown tired of. The drugs don't work anymore, and he has lost his edge. His world is not a place to show weakness, and as he loses his grip and his loved one is threatened, will Tate prove to be his saviour?

'IN DEEP' is a fast paced, gritty story, told from two perspectives. Set beneath the heat of the Spanish sun, with twists and turns as treacherous as the mountain roads.

This book is dedicated to my Mum, who encouraged me to write and urged me to believe in myself.

How you are missed, every day.

Bill

Bill returned to his shiny red car, as his body temperature soared, and perspiration clung to his forehead. He climbed into the scorching leather interior. Sweat bled from his pores and soaked his linen shirt. He cringed at the feel of the soggy material against his skin and fought the urge to peel it off. If Tate had not distracted him before he left home earlier, he would not have been late and forced to take the last parking spot beneath the relentless sun. His mind fought the urge to replay the feel of her wet, naked skin fresh from the pool.

The air conditioning kicked in as he pulled away and his breath slowed. He had this; he was in control. The bulging brown envelope stuffed with used notes, tucked safely beneath the passenger seat, ensured he would no longer answer to Tony.

"Pick your side Bill, do this one last job for me. If you keep the money, we carry on. But pass the payment my way- we're done – for good this time. And then you'd better watch your back." Tony's threat was real and replaying it made Bill doubt everything, but only for a second. This was no time for hesitation or weakness. He headed towards the west of town. It was almost siesta time, and the roads were quiet. If he played the next hour right, he could complete their final transaction and be back enjoying a cold beer in his pool within the hour. He just needed to hold his nerve.

The sprawling Andalusian villa, which Tony had purpose-built to accommodate his depraved needs, sat safely behind ornate powerful gates. This home belonged to a someone with money, who lived a luxurious life and to some extent, that part was true. Tony prided himself that his place was impenetrable. The most common story told about this was of the two petty criminals, who chanced their way from town to town, leaving a trail of thefts behind them. They foolishly once 'had a go' at Tony's. They made it over the wall, but never made it out again. Tony laughed and told everyone that he had sent them to 'work' with the pigs at one of his properties. They all knew what that meant.

On arrival he leaned through his window towards the intercom, "It's me, Bill."

There was no answer, simply a click followed by the steady opening of the electric gates. The driveway was wide enough for two cars and swept past a stone fountain surrounded by palms. Varying sized terracotta pots containing cacti and palms, peppered the edge all the way up to the imposing door. The lack of burly security guards was a façade - you just needed to know where to look. They watched everyone. He witnessed their brutality on those who 'stepped out of line', frequently. No one arrived here uninvited or left without being let go.

Bill slowed and swung right, around to the shade of the carport, and after switching off the engine he took a deep breath, reached onto the back seat and grabbed a freshly laundered shirt. As he stood up and unbuttoned his top, he caught a silhouette in the window of the guest accommodation above the pool area. Someone was watching him, as he mopped his torso with his removed shirt and popped the clean one on. He checked his reflection in the car window and whilst smoothing down his hair, tried to get a clearer view of whom it was, but the blind slammed shut.

His physique took more effort these days, but he could still turn heads. His dark hair and olive skin meant he was often mistaken for a native - his Spanish was excellent, but he was a British boy, born and bred. As a child, people commented about the little dark boy and seemed surprised that he was related to his blonde brother. He hated that. He felt like he did not belong, even then.

Grabbing the envelope and heading past the main house, he waved casually at the gardener who was busy pool cleaning with a toothless smile. He was on Tony's pay roll and subsequently did not just look after the pool and garden, he also had to keep his mouth shut and ignore all the crazy shit that went on daily.

Squeals and laughter resonated from the office area, separate to the main house and situated at the back of the pool.

Views from the side of the property were both mountain and sea in the far distance. Official 'business' was conducted there but not solely of the monetary kind, this was where the fun happened. As he got closer his mind flashed back to the crazy, hedonistic times, he had enjoyed off his head.

There was no invite to today's gathering, and for a moment, this bothered him, but clutching the envelope under his arm, he knew why. He was no longer in favour and there would be no more freebies for him from Tony. His breathing sped up, but this was no time for nerves. His inner voice advised him to stay calm and reminded him that the weak often end up floating face down in someone else's swimming pool. He puffed himself up, clicked his knuckles as though preparing for a fight and exhaled hard.

Through the archway into the courtyard, two indistinguishable blondes with differing bikinis, playfully chased one another around a large, tiled table. They could pass as twins, but that was due to a variety of cosmetic procedures. Their trademark was a promise of double trouble, and they did everything together. Everything. Tony liked having them around. Like fake designer goods, which at first glance look pucker but the closer you look the cheaper they appear- that was these two. He knew this from experience but in his defense, they seemed hotter the more powder you sniffed up your nose. Viv always wore red and Leila, blue.

The sacrificial table, round which they romped, was strewn with empty gin bottles and trails of white powder. Leila screamed as Viv held her skimpy bikini top above her head and as Bill unintentionally kicked a fallen bottle, their heads whipped around towards him. They licked their lips.

"Bill! It's been ages," Leila sauntered towards him and pressed her almost naked body against him. Her fingers traced slow circles on his neck, and she whispered in his ear, "Can you spare us five minutes?"

He turned his head away; Viv perched on the edge of the table; her legs spread wide. Bill grabbed Leila's arm and pushed her away. "He wants it rough today Viv, we can arrange that Bill." They crossed their arms above their heads in submission.

Bill raised his hand, "Not today, where's the boss?" Not so long ago he would have had these two without a second thought.

"Losing your edge, eh? Or perhaps he has a little problem Leila," Viv muttered as she drooped her little finger and made a sad face.

Bill's face curled in disgust.

"Oh, just fuck off then Bill, you never were much good at it anyway," she said as she dipped her finger into the white powder and rubbed it into her gums.

He pushed through the rich curtain hanging in the doorway of 'the office', decked out like a Moroccan Palace with blue and white tiles, rich scarlet fabrics and gold. Oversized lamps with gilded edges stood around the vast space and swung from the ceiling above a patchwork of plush sofas. Tony lent against a floor to ceiling mirror, watching the reflection of several naked women groaning on his sofa. His head flicked slightly as he sensed Bill's arrival and he clapped his hands before shoo-ing them away. The girls retrieved their individual skimpy items and disappeared through a door. Bill turned away. Soberness lit the seedy scene like a neon. He felt pity for the girls. He was going soft, losing his edge just like Viv said.

"Bill," Tony nodded.

"Tony."

They shook hands. Tony wiped away Bill's greeting on his shorts and lifted a whiskey glass to his mouth.

"So, Bill. This is it then, you've made your decision. Do I need to count it, or can I trust you?" He laughed but Bill felt his cold eyes pierce his skull.

"Your choice, but I've never screwed you over before. So, I guess we're done then." Bill sounded more confident than he felt.

Tony smiled and threw the bulging envelope onto the freshly abandoned sofa.

Bill wanted to leave quickly but made himself silently count to 10. He refused his mouth the urge to fill the silence. His instruction was to deliver the money, and leave, with minimal words. On his silent count of 10, he walked towards the door.

"Hey, Bill. You know the worst thing you ever did? Make the decision to work for him over me."

Bill kept on walking. Nothing he could say would satisfy Tony; it would just bring more trouble. That was a threat; Tony would not let him go that easily.

Bill just brokered a transfer deal of himself, from one depraved boss to another. There wasn't much to celebrate.

His sweat was not from the heat this time. Viv and Leila were now laying naked on loungers in sunglasses, and as he approached, they both turned onto their stomachs, away from him. He deliberately slowed his walk; breathed deeply.   He must look in control, but his legs were ready to bolt.

He needed a stiff drink. The figure in the window above the pool caught his eye again as he opened the car door, but the hazy sunshine blurred the reflection. God only knew who was watching him. He drove slowly, determined to appear calm but could not relax until he was the other side of those gates. Turning up the air conditioning, he wiped his brow with the back of his hand. His car slowed to a crawl and then stopped, "Fuck, please open, come on." Bill felt naked and exposed- a sitting duck. After a minute, the gates opened and allowed him to pass.

Rounding the corner onto the main road, he sped up and put as much distance as he could between him and Tony before he stopped and lit up a cigarette.

Jesus, since packing the in drugs, he really was losing his edge. His shaking hands stilled to a slight tremor as he drew the smoke deep into his lungs. Foreboding lingered around him like the stench of death, and he knew that Tony let him leave too easily.

He texted Tate: **You still at mine? Need some company. Back soon.**

Tate was his favorite of all the girls, eager to please and always available. Paying for company was easier than forming ties. She even offered him freebies and was happy to follow his instructions. It made it more fun without all the emotional bullshit women brough to his table.

He headed to Bar Caminos, and on arrival Paul beckoned him over, "You finished? Is it done?"

Bill nodded. It had been a long time coming.

"Two of the same," Paul ordered. The barman silently put together two whiskeys on ice with a dash of ginger. Paul passed one to Bill, chinked the glass with his own, and downed it, "another two," he ordered again, pointing with his fingers.

Bill lit up a cigarette and sunk into the armchair opposite Paul. He threw back his head and inhaled the smoke. He was tired. Tired of this whole thing and ready to disappear. The deal was complete, but nothing would really change for him; he was still working for a lunatic. Just a different one.

"You need to get your shit together. You could end up costing me, big time."

Bill jolted, could Paul now read his mind? Were even his private thoughts on the payroll?

"I'm good Paul. I just didn't get much sleep...bloody air-con packed up last night." What a shit excuse, but it was the only thing that sprung to mind.

Paul stared. "Well make sure of it. The word is that you're going soft. That what you want out there? Get your shit together." Paul dragged on the last of his cigarette and dropped it in the ashtray, "Come on I'm hungry, let's get some food. I know just the place."

Bill left his whiskey on the bar and cricked his stiff neck to one side, then the other. He took a breath and followed Paul through the bar door and into his shiny car. Tate would wait for him. She was a good girl, he thought as he sped out of town.

"Two tight little pieces of arse, waiting for us right now at the restaurant. A fun night awaits us my friend, so put your foot down," Paul instructed.

"Great." Bill lied, "Just what I need."

Tate

Tate squeezed her freshly conditioned hair and wrapped in it a towel before smearing moisturiser all over. The luxury of Bill's place was heaven compared to her own tiny dim room. When Bill called, she was always happy to drop everything, and he was generous with all he had. When she first met him, he was like all the others, with a chip on his shoulder and a disdain for women. Women were possessions to him and dispensable, but even then, she felt drawn to him.

His list of women was dwindling, and he seemed to text her more. She recently stopped picking up his payments and so it felt more like a relationship than an exchange of services. Most of the time she got sole use of his villa and his individual attention. She was sure it was changing; *he* was changing, and it was more than just 'business', these days.

She grabbed his robe from the back of the bathroom door and wrapped it around before picking up the I-pad. Being at Bill's place, meant she could call home, her mobile credit could never stretch that far. Outside she topped up her half-empty champagne glass and sunk into the recliner. This was her favourite spot for face timing her mum and she dialled the number with anticipation.

"Mum? Hi! How are you? How's Bella?"

"Darling, you look wonderful! Look at your tan, are you at Richards? Don't worry Bella is here too aren't you baby Bella?" Her mum reached down and lifted into view a tiny fluffy spaniel, which licked her face and jumped out of shot.

"Aww, I miss you both!" Tate face flushed with love. Richard was the name she created for Bill. She did not want to risk her mum knowing anything real about her life in Spain.

"Are you ok? What you up to? Looks like you're living the life of luxury!"

"I'm just about to make dinner for Richard, he'll be home soon, he's just texted actually! Our housekeeper has left us something to heat up." He had messaged her just as she got back home from his place, but she was happy to return, and Irena begrudgingly dropped her off at the villa. Even Irena's lectures about Bill, couldn't extinguish the excitement of him wanting her back again, so she decided to nod along and promise to think about ending whatever 'it' was she and Bill had going, rather than engage in it.

"Oh, that does sound nice, but darling I was just on my way out when you called, and my lift is waiting outside. Can we speak tomorrow? Will you call tomorrow? Promise?"

Tate fought her disappointment, "Sure mum, I promise. Have a great time, who's picking you up?"

"Oh no one, just a friend. I love you, enjoy your meal."

"Bye, love you." Tate ended the call and wiped her eyes. She did not expect her mum to be sulking at home and pining for her, but she felt a little dejected. She downed the last of her champagne.

Two hours passed since her phone pinged with Bill's text, she poured another glass and slipped off her robe. The intense sun warmed her skin, and she threw the towel from her head, onto the table close by, and tied a high knot into her hair. As she climbed into the Jacuzzi, she noticed how desperate for a manicure she was. Her lack of funds did not afford this luxury at present. Bill would notice and question her and then he would try to force his money onto her. She would have to repaint them. Her hair was easy to disguise as she could pin it up and hide the split ends, but her nails were a mess. The water felt good, her nails could wait until later.

She stretched out her legs one at a time in front of her, and pointed her toes, swirling the water with her feet. If this was her home, she could look after him- bring that elusive smile to his face. He often smiled, but she knew the difference between a genuine beam and one that stopped at the corner of his mouth. She wanted the real smile, the one that reached his eyes. Her latest fantasy was setting up home with Bill and she was working hard to make him need her, to turn it into her reality.

The jets pounded her aching muscles; her body tingled. She was ready for Bill's return and knew what his intentions would be. The champagne was light and refreshing, her glass soon empty again. She climbed out of the hot tub towards the outdoor fridge. A gentle mountain breeze tickled her naked, bronzed skin and she marvelled, just for a moment at the view. Uninterrupted vast mountains, peppered with white villas peeking out between the troughs of land. The cobalt sea reassuringly in the distance. It was heaven. Her mum would die for this, perhaps one-day Bill would even insist that her mum live here with them, "Tate," he would say, "You must bring Eileen here with us...this place is too big just for you and me. She can be your company when I'm too busy..." A warm glow rose to her cheeks and then dissipated with the ring of the house phone. Who was she kidding? She was living in dream world. Tate dripped across the tiled floor and picked up the ringing phone, convinced it would be Bill.

"Hey! Where are you?" The phone clicked off and she stared for a moment before placing it down. That was never a good thing. In films, those calls always preceded something sinister. Goose bumps sent chills across her body, and she hoped Bill would soon be back. Unease crept over her like a dark shadow. She knew Bill worked in a questionable world. Their paths crossing was less than conventional, and this was no cheesy love story. She was his hooker. That was a fact. She swallowed hard. "You do not count as a hooker if you aren't getting paid. I am not his hooker," she whispered and rubbed her neck shaking loose her hair.

WHEN BILL's car pulled up the drive, it was almost ten and her nails were dry and shiny. He wobbled slowly towards her, looking done in, but only to the expert eye. She was an expert on Bill. She loved to watch him, especially the way his face relaxed while he slept. That was the only time he was ever truly Bill. After all, you cannot maintain pretence when unconscious. Now he was home she could look after him and poured them both a whiskey. He liked it straight but on ice, no mixers and especially not ginger. That taste reminded him of a bad experience he had as a kid, he told her once while he was hammered. He moaned to her about how 'they' always ordered him whiskey with ginger - and how much he hated it. However, that was dangerous talk. You did not say things aloud about Tony or Paul. He never mentioned it again.

"Hey you." Bill slid his arms around Tate's waist and kissed her lips.

He tasted of whiskey, "Bill, you're too drunk to have driven. You know how that scares me. One day they'll find you off the edge of the mountain."

"Shhh." He put his finger to his lips. "You're not my Mum. You are not the Police," He shook his head slowly, "and I'm a big boy you know." He pushed her hand to his groin, "See."

She smiled. He needed her. His mouth was on hers, hungrily seeking her tongue. She happily complied and wrapped her legs around him. He picked her up, carried her to the table and slipped off his trousers. His fingers trailed from the tip of her neck to the curve of her breast. She arched her back and moaned. He was hers, just for that moment and she wanted to keep it that way.

As Bill took a shower, Tate picked up his clothes from the floor, buoyed by his homecoming. Her smugness instantly evaporated, as she put his shirt to her face to inhale his scent. Bill's usual citrus aftershave, mingled with the smell of alcohol, tobacco and sweet, cheap perfume. Her mood shifted. He had been with some other woman before he came home. Tears pricked at her eyes and her chest juddered with sobs, which threatened to choke her. She padded into the bathroom and threw all his clothing except for the evidence into the laundry. Bill finished his sobering shower and began drying himself off, unaffected by the sullen Tate who stared from the doorway.

"Who was she?" Tate sat on the stool by the bath and spoke softly, unsure if she wanted an answer. Her hands rung the delicate material of his shirt in her lap.

"Huh?" Bill rubbed his hair with the small towel, a larger one wrapped around his taut waist.

"Before you came home to me...who was she?" She threw the shirt at his feet and watched as it absorbed water from the wet floor. "I can smell her on it."

Bill looked to the floor and realised it was the shirt he had just removed. He shook his head, his face contorted into a grimace, "It's late, I'm tired and this is fucking ridiculous Tate." He threw the smaller towel onto the countertop and looked in the mirror, his deep breathing unnerved her. Perhaps she had gone too far.

"SHE was no-one," irritation carried his words. He scooped up the wet shirt and wrung it out in the sink before depositing it in the laundry basket. "I don't need to explain myself to you. Remember that. Remember why you are here, and the job you are paid to do." A dripping tap echoed around the bathroom. Bill turned the tap hard until it stopped. Silence bore down on her. She traced the line of the tiles with her freshly painted toes and prayed for him to break the uncomfortable silence. If ever she felt like a whore, it was in that moment.

"Paul set up some women at the restaurant."

Tate blinked back the tears and looked up at him. She rubbed her forearm. Why did he text her, make sure she was at his place? She hated games and refused to play them. Suddenly being naked felt awkward so she stood up

16

and tugged at the robe hanging on the back of the door. Pulling it over her, she turned away. Bill caught her hand and pushed her hard into the wall. The robe sank to the wet floor and marble tiles felt cold against her breasts.

"I told you. SHE was no one. She got nothing from me, despite all her efforts. Paul let me leave him to it and I came back here. I could have had her. But I didn't." He spoke slowly into her ear, "But I do not need to explain myself to you Tate."

He was always so damn in-control. Water dripped from his hair and trailed down her shoulders and back. She twisted her head round, but his eyes gave nothing away. If only she could tell him, how she loved him with every inch of her body. He was perfect to her, apart from his job, but he wasn't really *one of them*. He was a good soul. Somewhere inside, he was a good man.

Bill took hold of her other arm, spun her to face him, and held it above her head. At first, he kissed her gently, then deeper and he pulled her into the cavernous shower and pushed on the cool jets which dripped over their joined bodies. He came home to *her*. That was what he said. He chose *her*. Perhaps there was some hope, perhaps he was falling for her...

Bill

Tate lay sleeping, shrouded like a corpse, in a white sheet. Bill slipped into his shorts and headed to the kitchen to make coffee. His head pounded. Tony still haunted his thoughts. He would not let go that easily, it was all too easy. He did not want to end up like Phillippe. Phillippe tried to get out, but a week later, tourists found his car at the bottom of 'Death-valley'. His car and body-reduced to charcoal, along with the immediate vicinity. The newspapers reported him as a 'drunk-driver', a 'risk-taker'. Both could easily be true, but they knew the truth. That truth was Tony.

He took his steaming expresso out onto the terrace and sat beneath the shade. The sun was already beating down hard but his Ray bans filtered the glare from his jaded eyes. Bubbling jets of the infinity pool and the clicking of the Cicadas eased the silence.

He flicked through his phone and checked in on his daughter on her social media account. The images of her pouting and flirting in selfies were like needles through his heart. Gone was his chubby toddler, pestering for a carry. Comments, mainly from testosterone-fuelled teens, raised his blood pressure. He knew how their minds worked, and the thought of them and their grubby mitts all over his daughter, Ellie, was unbearable. He was in another country far away and could do nothing but push down his bubbling

18

anger to a simmer. One day he would show them, and he burned their images into his mind for a later date.

She was busy enjoying Glastonbury, thanks to him. He managed to acquire her four tickets, through a contact, and a selfie of her and three pretty mates smiled at him with a 'Thanks #superdad'. His gesture was pitiful compared to the years he missed-out on her life, but he was glad she was having fun, even if her vest was too low-cut for his liking.

He drained the last of his coffee and wandered across the freshly swept terrace. Maria had been over before he had awoken and tidied. His house would be a tip without his housekeeper. Suddenly he realised that Tate's car was not in the drive. She must have got a taxi over, which was strange. He took off his shades and pinched the bridge of his nose- perhaps a swim would clear his head.

His skin relished the cool silky water as he swam to the bottom of the pool. Sometimes he felt as though he spent his life underwater trying to get back up to the surface for air. Two feet appeared, dangled over the edge and he swam towards them, tugged at them and surfaced to hear Tate scream.

"Stop it! I've got a coffee in my hands!" She kicked him away and he pushed off from the side on his back completing a final two lengths.

"Did you sleep well?" she asked as he climbed the pool steps.

"Uh-huh. You?"

"Yep. Always do here. It's so peaceful. You want more coffee?"

"No, juice please," he rubbed his face and neck with his towel. "Where's your car? Did you get a taxi here?"

"No. Irena dropped me here," she turned away.

"Why?" Bill lent against the wall.

"Why what?"

"Why did she drop you? Why didn't you drive here?" He spun her round to face him. Why was she lying to him?

Tate brushed him off and sat on one of the loungers with her face to the sun.

"Tate? Why are you ignoring me? Where is your car?" His voice raised as he moved to block her sun. She nursed the hot coffee in her hands.

"It's nothing. Really." She picked at a loose thread of the stripy lime cushion.

"Okay. I'm gonna ask you again, and this time you'll answer me. Tate where is your car?"

She pulled harder and the thread snapped.
"Repossessed. My car got repossessed Bill." Her cheeks burned and she swung her legs off the sun lounger and headed towards the kitchen.

Sometimes he forgot that money was a problem for people, ironic considering the lack of it around in his childhood years. He followed her into the kitchen and reached into his wallet that lay on the work surface. "Ok. I'll sort it."

"NO! No, you won't Bill. I don't want you to. I told you I do not need you to pay me. I am here because I want to be here…"

Was that a pang of guilt, right there in his chest? When did he last pay her? He thought hard and couldn't remember. Her freebies were ongoing. The trouble was- if he was no longer responsible for paying her wage, and yet she seemed to spend most of her time with him, how was she paying her bills?

"Listen, I expect you to be here when I call you. How can you if you don't have a car? I said I will sort it and I will." It was true, and he did want her to be available, so a car was the least he could offer. It helped ease his guilt too. "I'm taking a shower and then I need to go out. You can stay here, or I can drop you off somewhere. It's your choice but I want you to take this money. You can't live on fresh air." He did not wait for her response.

21

The cold shower took his breath away but awakened his senses. What the fuck was he doing not paying her after everything he knew about women. He was just encouraging her to think there was more to this than there was. He shook his head, disappointed in his own lack of judgement and determined to put things right. She needed to go back onto his payroll, like it or not.

Tate

Tate drew her legs into her chest and hugged them tight. Instead of Bill dropping her off somewhere, she stayed at the villa- her dingy apartment and the ever-growing pile of outstanding bills could wait. Tears of self-pity clouded her shades. Were the tears because she was skint, for her unrequited love or the small fact that she was a whore? All three were individual reason enough, for tears.

Being a prostitute was never part of her life plan and she hid it from her family back home, her regular video calls from the villa were enough to fool them. When she had landed at Malaga airport three years before, she carried only a case of clothes and make-up. She also brought with her determination to make her dream come true of building a new life for herself.

The year prior to arriving, she scrimped and saved her money as she planned her new life. She longed to spread her wings and show her Mum that she could be someone; go somewhere. Her Mum never had the opportunity to go far and bringing Tate up alone meant money was always in short supply. Eileen was in awe of her brave daughter, moving abroad. She urged Tate to learn some Spanish before embarking; it would help her to get a better job. However, Tate argued that she would learn it quicker by living in the country; be fluent within a few months. Eileen knew how determined her daughter was and when to let go, and their conversation concluded with eye rolling on both sides.

Tate swallowed hard, how had she sunk so low? The look of horror on her mum's face if she ever found out would be utterly heart-breaking. She would never have met Bill if her life had not have run so out of control, but she would also not be inflicted with the mental scars this line of work imposed on her. Her scars were deep and permanent; she was damaged. Now, sat in his beautiful villa, in luxurious surroundings, she knew things could be a lot worse for her.

It was months since she last 'worked' with the other men and she was determined that part was over, regardless of how she and Bill played out. Bill aside, her 'working girl' career was a short two months long. Two long, brutal months. Thank God Bill saved her.

On arrival in Spain, she loved her little bar job- meeting and coercing sun burned holiday makers in, with the promise of free shots and the best time guaranteed on the whole of the costa. Soon, she and the charmer head barman were shacked up and things were great for a short time. Late nights, long sleeps in the sun, cash in her pocket. But he was in debt with a local 'firm' who ended up selling on his debt to Tony's lot, and unfortunately, she caught their eye. Lean tanned and twinkling eyes were enough to put her on their radar.

She laid back on the soft cushion. A fluttering wad of notes caught her eye. Bill had put the champagne bottle cooler on top of them, to stop them blowing away. She flicked her head from the temptation of the money and focused on a trailing plant wound around the pergola, which was blowing gently in the wind.

She needed that money; her cupboards were empty, and she was behind on her rent with no way out. By now, she hoped to have moved into his villa, full time. If she took the money, she was still his whore and all her efforts to raise her status from that place, were for nothing. Her reputation would always taint her life. Maybe she could move away, where no one knew her and banish her dirty secret to the past. There she could concentrate on being the real Tate, the one she left in the UK. However, she could never leave Bill and his ties to the area ran deep.

If only they could leave forever and get a house near to his daughter, she would be a great step mum to her. Bill could be genuinely happy.

She closed her dewy eyes, and rested her body back on the lounger, tired from chasing thoughts around her mind. Sleep rescued her from negativity as her tears evaporated in the heat and she dreamed of children and parties on the terrace, with Bill.

THE FIRST blow to her head- sent her flying off the lounger. Dazed, was she dreaming? She rolled onto her back and opened her eyes as two figures loomed above her. They clawed at her robe and kicked her with their heavy-booted feet. She curled into the foetal position, "BILL!"

Who were they? They said nothing. The shorter one of the pair tugged hard at the robe belt as the other peeled it from her purpling skin. They laughed and jeered as she clung to her clothing, kicking and smacking away their hands. They were too strong, and she was soon exposed.

"Take whatever you want...I know where there's money...I can give you money...please..." Her puce face feared their motives as she fought hard, lashing whenever a limb was free. They laughed and again the shorter one grabbed at her naked body, pinching and prodding her flesh. "It's not your money we want." He licked his lips and drool dribbled down his chin.

"Get off me, HELP Maria!" she shrieked, hoping her screams would carry over to Maria's house, "Get the fuck off me!"

He lowered his face to hers squeezing her chin between his dirty fingers. She could smell the stench of his breath as he spoke, "Shut your fucking mouth, everyone knows you're a dirty whore!" His words stung as hard as any blow, and she spat in his face. He wiped her spit from his cheek and slapped her hard before bearing down on her mouth. She could not breathe with the force of his disgusting kiss and his rough tongue choked her.

The taller one stamped on her hand and held his foot there. "I'll hold her down and you go first."

She gasped for air as her freed mouth gagged. He unzipped his trousers and began licking her pinned down thighs. She struggled to free her legs, but he bit her in retaliation and her screams echoed as he sunk his teeth. The table behind them overturned in the chaos and the banknotes Bill left fluttered around them like confetti. A glistening caught her eye. Just near her free hand, beside the overturned table, lay a smashed champagne bottle, and just within reach was a shard, small enough to hold but big enough to injure. She grabbed it and her hand bled from its sharp edge, then she lay still, as if passed out. The biting stopped. Her aggressor slowly moved up her body, leaving a slimy trail with every lick. "It's okay, you don't need to be awake for this," he laughed. "This one is on the house, eh?" he smiled through decaying teeth. Tate's skin crawled with his touch. As he lowered his body onto hers, she sunk the broken glass into his neck, and he reeled backwards; his blood sprayed the white walls of the villa. The bigger man seized her matted hair and smashed her head into the terracotta tiling. As darkness consumed her world, the panicked screams of the injured man filled the silence...

Bill

The church bell chimed eleven and the plaza buzzed with families enjoying breakfast; their chattering echoed around. Bill nodded towards three elderly men, sat on their bench, beneath the shade of the church. They wiled their mornings away discussing the latest news and shaking their heads at the youth of today. He headed towards the café on the far side; a covering of multi-coloured umbrellas shaded the tables beneath.

"Antonio? Café solo," he sat down and sparked up a cigarette. It was his regular table and afforded a view of the entire square. A stray emaciated dog, sat like stone beside a breakfasting family, hoping for scraps. He hated seeing that. There was plenty of them around, especially when the cooler evening arrived.

From the church door, a cocoa-skinned woman appeared in a white lace ankle-length dress. She paused in the doorway, tucked a strand of hair behind her ear and placed an over-sized straw hat on top of her shoulder length curls. Antonio delivered Bill's coffee in silence.

He watched her meander across the cobbled square and settle at the table next to his. Antonio was beside her in a flash, "Senorita, please allow me." He tucked in her chair, "Shall I move this umbrella for you, would you like more shade?" He spoke in broken English and clearly thought his luck was in.

"Oh no, thank you, I'm enjoying the sunshine, besides I have this. "She laughed and pointed to her head. "I would like a water please sin... gas?"

"Si, senorita. Anything for such a beautiful lady." He bowed and smiled.

Bill beckoned him over with a flick of his head and leaned in close. "Cut it out Romeo, leave her alone. Whatever she orders, put it on my tab. You understand me?"

Antonio nodded, and sped off towards the kitchen, swearing under his breath.

Bill slowly drank his coffee whilst enjoying the newest attraction. Early 30s, maybe. No wedding band, English and nervous. She fanned her dress to cool down and gratefully received her water from the less-friendly waiter, who glanced towards Bill with a grimace. Bill suppressed his urge to laugh with a cough, which caught the attention of the woman, who smiled.

"Good morning."

"Oh, you're English! I thought you might be Spanish!" She smiled.

"It's very hot today," Bill's his eyes roamed beneath the safety of his shades.

"Yes, the church was cool but as soon as I stepped out, well the heat is so intense!"

He watched as she gulped down the water. Beads of moisture trailed her neck and disappeared under the bust of her dress.

"You're on holiday here?"

"Yes. It's lovely…but just so hot. I'm not used to it. England is usually cold! I don't know why I'm telling you that, you know how it is! Do you live here?"

"Uh-huh. Still miss it though. Maybe one day I'll go back, who knows?"

Her phone beeped and she retrieved it from her straw handbag.

"OH."

"Bad news?"

"Just my friend, can't meet me now. Not until later."

"I'm happy to show you around. My colleague is already half an hour late. So, I guess he's not coming either. I'm Bill and you are?" He stood beside her and held out his hand.

"Celia, hi Bill." She shook his hand gently. It felt soft and slender in his.

"Well Celia, how about a stroll and maybe some brunch? Have you eaten yet?"

"I haven't eaten, and I wouldn't usually wander off with some guy I just met. But I have a good vibe about you Bill. I suppose...I mean...I am on holiday, right?" She finished off her water and Bill threw down a twenty.

"I got it, its fine." He smiled, what happens in Spain, stays in Spain, seemed to be the rule when holidaying and that made casual sex easy to obtain.

"Thanks." Celia stood and smoothed down her dress.

"Antonio, Hasta Luego!" he laughed and waved dismissively. Antonio scowled, as Bill and Celia strolled away. He decided to head for the Terrace Bar, which afforded an impressive view across the rooftops and would excite any new arrival. With his hand on the small of her back, he guided her gently down the shaded passageways of the ancient white town.

"Oh, it's beautiful. I LOVE it here!" She gushed pointing to the wooden doors, framed with Moroccan inspired tiles, and terracotta pots crammed with flowers and plants. Seeing her so enthused brought a smile to his face.

"I suppose it is," he answered.

A roar echoed down the narrow street as a young lad on a Vespa sped up behind them. Bill threw Celia against the wall and narrowly avoided a collision with the speeding motorcycle, "You okay?"

"I think so." Her heart pounded against his chest. He pulled away and took her hand to lead her on.

"You have to watch out; they seem narrow but are still used by bikes."

"Seems I have a lot to learn around here. I best be on my guard." She pulled her hand from his grip and shifted her handbag across to her other shoulder.

They turned right and then left before climbing a steep staircase up to an open-sided terrace. "Hey Drew, my usual if you please."

"Sure Bill, follow me please," the Canadian owner ended his telephone call and dashed around the reception desk.

"Bill, this is stunning." She shook her head and curls spilled out as she removed her hat. Immediately beneath the terrace was a maze of streets and terracotta roofs, the vast mountains and sea in the distance. Her hand rested on her throat as she drank in every detail.

"How you doing Bill?" Drew pulled out a chair and waited for Celia to sit, before pushing it in and unfolding a napkin onto her lap.

"Good thanks, can we have a bottle of water, two coffees and a selection of pastries to begin with."

"Sure. Some fruit juice?"

"Yes."

Off he scuttled towards the kitchen, as Bill removed his shades and leant back in his chair.

Celia snapped away with her camera. She seemed different.

"You married?"

She shook her head. "Was, he died. Last year. I've come out here for some 'me time'. A friend of mine lives out here- invited me over. So I jacked in my job and plan to be here for at least a month."

Bill digested what she just said. A widow. He had not had one of those before. A new challenge.

Drew arrived with a waitress, laid out their banquet and disappeared as quickly as they arrived.

"Wow, you sure know how to get good service round here."

"I have my uses." he winked, and Celia laughed. Her plump lips glistened with clear lip-gloss and beneath, her teeth were straight and white. "Coffee?"

"Hmm, thanks." He passed her a filled cup, and she chose a sticky Danish whirl. She licked her fingers after each mouthful. His guttural mind decided she was doing it on purpose.

"So, Bill, you married?"

"Was, a long time ago. Unfortunately, she didn't like the lifestyle out here and left. Took my daughter with her, eighteen now. Hard to believe, I know what you're thinking - I don't look old enough to have an eighteen-year-old daughter. It's been said many times before."

Celia laughed, "I would say you don't look a day older than 30."

It was her turn to wink and this time he laughed, all the way to his eyes.

BILL SPOKE into his hands-free. "Hey Paul? Why the no-show today?"

"Something came up."

"Are we talking business or women?" he laughed, buoyed by his hours spent with Celia. He had only managed a kiss goodbye, but he took her number and was hopeful it would not take too long for some action. She texted him within half an hour of their parting to thank him. His charm offensive paid off.

"Business, and your concern is too little too late, you been otherwise engaged no doubt. That little whore of yours keeping you busy?"

Bill winced. He said nothing. He learned early on, not to say too much, ever.

"Got news that Gina's was on the list for a raid. I had to clear up. Took V with me."

"Shit," Bill's mood slumped.

"Anyway, it's sorted...no thanks to you. V torched it and there's nothing to be found now. I gotta go, Faye's waiting for me, got some party to go to."

Bill clicked the remote for his gates and swung up the drive. He remembered he was supposed to order a car for Tate, but his encounter with Celia had distracted him. He could do it mañana. The gates closed behind him. He wandered round the back, threw his keys on the table and grabbed a beer from the outside fridge. Something was up. His hunch was not usually wrong. The house was unlocked but there was no sign of anyone. He lifted his shades onto his head, was that blood on the wall?

 "MARIA? TATE?" No answer.

He dumped his beer and ran around to the blood-splattered wall.

"Shit!" Tate's lifeless body lay face down next to clumps of hair on the tiles. Congealed blood trailed across the terrace. Her bruised naked body had taken a pounding.

Was she alive? He knelt beside her and felt for a pulse, "Thank fuck."

"Tate, I'm going to lift you into the house, can you hear me?" He gently carried her inside and laid her carefully onto his bed. Her rolling eyes struggled to focus. "NO! Please – leave me alone."

"Shh, Tate, it's me. Bill. You're safe." He stroked her swelling cheeks as his blood pressure rose like a volcano. His twisted face surveyed her battered body as she writhed on the bed, fighting off invisible aggressors before slipping unconscious again. He covered her shivering body to the neck with a sheet and took his phone from his pocket.

"Shaun, get hold of Joe and get round here quick. I need help with something."   He dialed again.

"Maria? Hi, no not a good day. No, just listen to me...can you come to the house right now, and is Adela home? She is - bring her too and her medic kit. Yes, as quickly as you can. No, I'll explain when you get here, it's Tate, and she's in a bad way."

Maria, his housekeeper, lived 2 minutes away and over the years proved herself trustworthy. Her mouth stayed shut no matter what she witnessed. Bill's villa played host to many a wild 'gathering'. Naked bodies, empty bottles, wraps, foils, whatever lay strewn at the villa, Maria simply 'worked around'. Her sorrowful eyes looked on him as a naughty wayward son, who would come-good in the end. Her daughter, Adela, was her pride and joy and was a qualified doctor, thanks to Maria using all her income from Bill to put her through university. Maria was grateful for her 'higher than average' wage. At least something good had come of all this, he thought as he waited their speedy arrival.

He paced the floor beside his bed, frustrated and helpless. Knowing hospital was not an option, he fought the guilt as it crept accusingly in, this was his fault. This was just the beginning.

Maria and Adela burst in, "What's going on?" Adela demanded.

"I came home and found her on the floor. She's breathing but in a bad way, she's been attacked judging by the bite marks."

"So, you weren't here when this happened?" Her eyebrows arched high on her forehead.

"No, I just said didn't I- for fucks sake. Stop judging me and fucking help her." Bill's voice rose and his fists clenched.

"Bill. Stop this. She is trying to help, and you are not making this better for Tate. Go fix yourself a drink." Maria gently pushed him towards the door.

He left the women tending to Tate and went out to speak to the boys, who had just pulled up. He still was not clear on exactly how far Tony's men had gone. Rape was not something he wanted on his shoulders again. Outside, Bill righted the fallen table before smacking the wall hard and letting out a guttural roar.

"What the fuck is going on Bill?" Shaun rounded onto the terrace, "Someone died?"

"Tate, she's bad. Reckon it was Tony, a clear message. Clean this place up, will you? Do it quietly and replace anything broken. I want it back to normal and get rid of that blood, probably going to need to paint the whole side. Then let's get some cameras fixed up, shall we? I think we're going to need them."

Bill strode to the kitchen where Maria filled the washing machine with blood-stained towels.

"Is she okay?"

"Not really, she's a mess but there's no sign of rape at least, she has suffered a great deal, Bill. She will need to stay here. I can help you to look after her...until she is recovered enough to leave."

Bill sighed and nodded, "Thanks Maria."

Adela emerged from his bedroom. Her face did not convey the same affection that her mother afforded him. "Here are some pain killers; she is going to need these regularly. I've already given her morphine for the pain, to get her started. You need to make sure she is kept clean, if she gets an infection, it will mean hospitalisation whatever your stupid rules say. I gave her a Tetanus shot too, for the bite marks. Mama, you can help, ensure she gets all this? I'm not going to waste my breath with my opinion, because I already know you are not informing the Police." Adela shook her head, "I only do this for my Mama and as for Tate, I just hope when she pulls through, she leaves this villa and never comes back."

"For your expenses," Bill pulled a wad of cash from his wallet and handed it to her.

She looked at the folded notes, "I will not be bought but I cannot leave this poor woman to suffer. I will take your money, but it will go to the Woman's refuge, you know, the place where abused women are cared for?" She snatched the dirty money from his hand.

Bill's cheeks flushed, "This wasn't me ...I didn't lay a finger on her..."

"Maybe you didn't. But there was a reason someone beat her, kicked her and BIT her. Anyway, I'm saying no more to you. Mama, I'm heading home." She kissed Maria on the cheek and squeezed her hand. Bill felt chastised, and no one else could have got away with that. He was glad the other two were busy outside and not witnesses. Weak. Wasn't that what Paul had said he was being called? He would have wiped the floor with Adela once upon a time. Bill scratched his neck and sighed.

"Shall I go in and see her?"

"She's sleeping, give her half an hour. I will take the boys some coffee." Maria took charge. Tate was her patient now.

Bill headed into the bathroom and peeled off his blood-stained clothes. His hands were stained red too, not for the first time in his life. His hands had worn the blood of many over the years. Somehow, her blood burned his skin. He looked at his reflection, he looked like shit. He scrubbed his hands in the sink and climbed in the shower. The shower jets pounded his head and shoulders. Guilt seemed to follow him around these days, like a stray dog begging for scraps. Tate's attack was in *his* home, as a warning to HIM, whilst he sat with Celia. This was just how Tony liked to play. He knew Tony let him go too easily.

Tate

"Mum? Is it you?" Tate's swollen eyes blurred her vision, but a gentle hand stroked her face.

"Shush my love, it's okay," Maria spoke in a whisper. "You are safe, you must rest."

Tears stung her face. It was not her mum's voice. Her puffy eyes blinked hard and her whole body throbbed. "Take this my love," Maria lifted Tate's head forwards, enough to enable a sip of water and popped in a pill to help ease the pain.

"Bill?" Tate squeezed the words from her split lips.

"No, he's working, but you are safe. I won't leave your side," Maria promised.

"What happened?"

"Rest now."

"Please tell me…"

"You were attacked. You've been badly hurt but now you must rest Tate."

Tate glanced to her left where she could just make out what looked like a battered woman, laying on a bed. Was she in hospital? "Where am I Maria?"

"You're at Bill's, in the guest room."

Her piercing scream cut through the quiet.

The battered woman was her own reflection.

"No, Tate, this is no good for you. You must calm down. Please?" Maria rhythmically stroked her hair with the very tips of her fingers, "Shh, it's okay."

Tate's screaming subsided to a sob. She turned her head back towards the mirror and forced herself to look at what she had become.

Bill appeared at the door, "Tate? What's happening? Are you in pain?"

"BILL! Oh Bill." Sobbing reduced her words to an inaudible mess. She wanted to reach out to him and pull his strong arms around her, but overwhelming pain engulfed her. She winced. Tears rolled down her face.

He knelt next to her head and gently kissed her swollen cheek. "So, you're back with us. You had us all worried for a while."

"How long have I been this way?" her hoarse voice cracked.

"Three days." She reached to her throat and rubbed it. Maria instinctively brought the water to her lips aided with a straw.

Tate laid her head back on the pillow. A fan positioned nearby, spun furiously to keep her cool.

"Maria has not left your bedside. You've received the best care you know." Bill whispered.

Two scruffy men flashed before her eyes, and she shook.

"What is it Tate? Are you remembering something?"

She nodded. "I think so. Two of them, they ripped off my robe...Bill...I can't remember what they did to me..." her voice rose to a shrill, "I can't remember, Oh no no no."

"Tate, stop. You're safe. I'm here for you. Maria's daughter, Adela, is a doctor, and she has examined you. She has treated your wounds. You weren't, they didn't..."

41

he lowered his voice, "they didn't rape you." He kissed her forehead gently.

Sobs racked her body, and every movement caused pain somewhere new. Bill stroked her hair until she fell back into an exhaustive sleep.

PAIN SEARED through Tate's ribs, the clock said 2am as she blinked her eyes into focus. The scent of the flowers filling her room reminded her of her Saturday job, in the floristry shop where her Mum worked, when she was young. She reached over to the bedside table for painkillers and glugged the water, kindly left by Maria, who had also left a dim nightlight on for her.

With care and control, Tate shuffled off the bed across the cold tiles towards the bathroom, dodging the vases of flowers everywhere. She acknowledged the gesture inwardly as to smile caused too much pain but as she lowered herself onto the toilet, her whimpers echoed around the bathroom.

"Tate, you ok?" Bill appeared in the doorway, dishevelled and sleepy. "You should have called me, I could have helped you," he yawned.

"I'm okay. I needed to pee."

Bill turned away, "Well let me help you back to bed at least when you're done."

Tate washed her hands and stared at her alien face in the mirror. "Don't look at me Bill, I'm hideous," she trembled and felt light-headed. Her knees sagged, and Bill leaned in to steady her.

"I'm getting you back into bed right now, you shouldn't try and get up without help, what if you fell and knocked yourself out?"

Bill lifted her up and gently carried her to the bed.

"Will you lay with me for a while? I don't want to be alone."

Bill climbed onto the bed and lay on his side to face her. His steady breath reassuringly warmed her cheek.

"Thanks for the flowers, they're beautiful," Tate's voice cracked, and her tears rolled onto the pillow. Bill grabbed a tissue from the side table and dabbed her eyes.

"You need sleep. I'm here, you're safe now. You need to save your energy to get back on your feet."

Tate closed her eyes. He was with her, would protect her. Sleep carried her back to her mum as they put together flowers for a wedding, amidst curling ribbons and the scent of lilies.

Bill

Bill swung his car into the underground carpark and took the stairs two at a time. He was late, the story of his life. Celia may have given up on him; he should have been there an hour ago. He arrived at the top of the stairs just as he spotted her heading out of the front door, "Celia!" She turned and tapped her watch with a smile. He cocked his head to the side and kissed her on both cheeks, "You look amazing."

"Bill, I'm in my gym gear. I hardly think so. You were supposed to meet me for a workout! I'm done already and you, well you're hardly dressed for the gym now are you?" She pointed to his open shirt, shorts and flip-flops. His messy hair and stubble only added to his raw appeal, he looked good close-shaved or not. Today was a casual day with no meetings booked and a lack of sleep because of Tate.

"Sorry, got caught up in some business..." He blocked the image of Tate's battered face. "How about a swim instead? Got swimmers on under these." He pointed to his shorts and smiled at the image of Celia in a swimsuit, which blinded him. Now that would soothe his addled brain.

"Well, I have my swim gear, so okay then. You're on!" Celia high-fived him and Bill grabbed a towel from behind the spa desk. They headed towards the pool, decorated like Roman baths, with oversized pots and plants around the edge. Huge columns separated poolside-seating areas and hot tubs bubbled alongside the steaming sauna in the corner. Empty, except for one another honeymooning couple, it was perfect timing.

Celia emerged from their separate changing areas and Bill's eyes widened. He swiftly entered the pool on sight of her one-piece, cut low to her navel. Her hair- scraped into a bun off her face, showcased her exquisite features. She glided into the pool from the side of the deep end and breast stroked towards him. He lent against the side of the pool and watched her every movement. He needed her. They had been texting back and forth for days. Her messages were warming up to his charm, and she was buying every compliment and trick he threw her way.

Guilt, flashed. Last time he was with Celia, Tate was almost killed. Paul was unprepared to do anything about Tony's attack. He wasn't starting a battle over a worthless hooker, even if it was aimed at Bill. "Go for a retaliation if that's what you need Bill, but you're on your own with it – I've got enough going on right now and you aren't pulling your weight as it is. Thin ice mate, that's where you are." He was in danger of losing everything, including his reputation if he let it go. But without Paul behind him, it wasn't worth risking. Tony knew that and she was just a hooker after all...

45

"I thought we were swimming, not skulking in the shadows?" Celia splashed water into his face and laughed.

Bill pulled her close, "Hey, skulking is my speciality and that's just asking for trouble…" he splashed her face and grabbed her hand and kissed it, then her wrist, elbow, and peppered her shoulder, before holding her head in his hands and kissing her mouth. Jesus, what was this woman doing to him? She pulled back and looked straight into his eyes, "Easy tiger!"

A brunette with a clipboard called to the honeymooners, it was time for their massage. Celia swam to the edge of the pool and Bill watched her toned body climb out and head to the sauna. He waited a moment and followed her inside anticipating her next move.

The heat shortened his breath as steam from the coals choked the chamber. Her hand found his shoulder and she kissed his back and neck, circling him but refusing him control of the situation. Each time he reached out to touch her, she firmly moved his hand back to his side. Gentle nibbles to his ear sent shivers all over his body; still she kept his hands, down. Lingering kisses took her from his neck, chest and down to his stomach. He arched his back in expectation and let out a sigh.

The door opened wide. A large man in a tiny pair of shorts huffed and puffed his way in through the steam. The moment was gone. Celia squeezed Bill's arm, and Bill muttered. He wanted to kill that man. On the plus side, he now knew she was up for it and he would not have to wait long. They headed out towards the changing rooms. The widow was worth the wait. He could wait.

The juice bar at the spa was modern and cool. There was a vast picture window displaying the distant mountains, and it was in front of this floor to ceiling view where they sat.

"That was a surprise." Bill raised his eyebrows.

"What the tiny shorts that the man wore?" she winked.

"I think you know exactly what I mean."

Celia blushed and smiled coyly. "I don't know what happened in there, must be the heat."

"Don't apologise. What are you up to for the rest of the day?"

"Well, sunbathing and lunch with Flavia then an afternoon of reading my book by her pool."

Bill's phone rang, "Sorry, I really have to get this." He stood up and walked away, it was Paul.

"Bill, I need you at Caminos in ten." He did not wait for an answer and Bill re-pocketed his phone. Celia looked up from her phone whilst sucking on her straw.

"I have to go. I'm sorry."

"I thought you weren't working today?"

"Me too. Perhaps we can meet up again soon?" He did not want to let this one stray too far. If he was not on the scene, she would soon be picked-up by some low-life waiter.

"Sure. I'd love to. How about you text me next time you're free?" Bill leant in and double kissed her, lingering for a second, they lightly brushed lips. It took every ounce of his strength to pull away and leave.

"I'll be in touch soon," he whispered and then headed out, down the stairs and into his cool car, grateful for the shaded underground carpark.

CAMINOS, a dark dated bar with wood panelled walls inside and two huge barrels to stand at, out front. The bar was well stocked and the tapas cheap but tasty. The wall lights were brown glass and mounted on wooden holders, beneath which hung paintings of the mountains and various cacti. The air hung heavy with cigarette smoke. It was full of the usual crowd but sweat seeped across Bill's top lip as he sensed something going down.

Paul glanced at his watch. "You been nursing that whore? No, hold on...left her home with hired help and out shagging some other bit of skirt...tut, tut."

Bill laughed and fought the urge to knock Paul's teeth through the back of his head, "Good one boss."

"Drink? Whiskey, ginger and ice for my friend. Make it a large. He's gonna need one." Paul slapped his back a little too hard. Bill winced but smiled through gritted teeth. He was tired of this façade. He took the drink from the bar and gulped half down, fighting a grimace from the sting of ginger. "You want to speak to me, something new?"

"Yes, not in here. Follow me." Paul ushered him out the back, past the first stock room filled with stacked crates of bottles. Through a panelled door, the back room had a huge window with a view of a walled courtyard, empty except for a lone pushbike. Floor to ceiling shelves lined the walls.

"Cigarette?" Paul took two from his pack and lit them both, handing one to Bill. He lent against the wall and concentrated intently on blowing out smoke-rings. Bill stared at the damp patch on the wall above Paul's head and imagined smashing his head against it. He wished they would all just leave him alone; he didn't know if he had it in him anymore.

"So, since talk of Gina's raid, I have been reliably informed that we can no longer operate as we were. I believe one of our lot is spilling information to Tony, who is in turn informing the authorities. We need to be clever. It's time to switch operations. Instead of holding - we're importing. Right now, they're cleaning out all our holding areas, not a trace of evidence left. They can raid what they like because they'll find nothing. We'll lay low, whilst the raids happen and then in a month or two, we begin again."

Bill knew what was coming. He dropped his dog-end to the floor and flattened it. He put his hands into his pockets and faced Paul.

"Only this time, we use people, females, desperate for money. You will use your charm, your reassuring nature to recruit young women. Invite them on a holiday of a lifetime in peaceful Andalucía. We can buy a villa set up a holiday home, a taxi service from the airport even. Initially of course, we will use real holidaymakers, families, couples. The word will spread, and the business accepted as legitimate. Then we begin. We use it to bring in the drugs via Africa. We use different transport – mix it up, planes and ferries. Days out to big cities, where my contacts are already established. Then the girls can sit back and enjoy the rest of their holiday. It's win, win."

Bill's stomach churned; his mind pictured his smiling daughter with her friends at Glastonbury. Innocent young girls, tempted by free holidays and he would carry more guilt, responsible for their corruption, imprisonment, maybe even death. He couldn't do it, but he knew what would happen if he said no. "You make it sound so easy…"

"There's no reason it shouldn't be…we just need to find some willing girls." Paul pushed away from the wall and at an inch taller than Bill, spoke down to him, smiling. "But you have time. As I said, we need to get the legitimate business up and running first and I have my solicitor onto this already."

Bill nodded and stepped back.

"You know any willing young women Bill?"

"No, I don't like them too young. Some of the others…they do…"

"No Bill. This is between you and me."

 Bill fumbled through his pockets for a cigarette, "Leave it with me for now."

"I knew you'd see sense. You owe me Bill. I took a leap of faith bringing you back from Tony."

Bill nodded under Paul's glare. They left the light of the back room and made their way through the throng of raucous men, shouting and leering at the big screen, where a pole dancer was busy advertising some dodgy late-night channel.

Bill sat at the bar and ordered tapas. His stomach grumbled. He tucked into the variety of flavours and ordered a cold beer to wash it down. "How's the family?" He asked the barman, Jose.

"Good, thanks." Bill imagined he got little time with them, as he was always open for Paul and his cronies. This incessant guilt which was seeping into his core would be his death. He did not like it. He was part of this chaotic life, which caused men to lose their families. His own lonely, pitiful existence was a prime example and he was nearer the top of the food chain than Jose. Bill had all that money could buy, except peace of mind. He finished off his food and left Jose a €50, larger than usual, to appease the stomach-churning remorse, or perhaps it was the beginnings of an ulcer. Either way, his life was seven shades of shit.

Tate

Tate sat out by the pool. The freshly painted terrace bore no trace of her attack, but she still felt uneasy. It was not her first beating. In her line of business, thrashings were always a risk – prostitutes were worthless to most people and deserved whatever they got. She just needed a little time, to heal emotionally. The warmth of the sun on her face was a tonic, and she was glad to be free of her bed. Maria fussed around and brought her a cushion to put behind her sore back, coffee and a croissant, "Here put these sunglasses on."

Maria pulled out the chair opposite and sat down. "Ok, now tell me, what are you doing here?"

Tate's puzzled face stared at her, "You know why, you're looking after me."

"No, that's why you are here right this moment; I asked you what you are doing *here*? It's totally different."

Tate sipped her coffee and contemplated the question, "Because I love him."

Maria shook her head, "Not a good enough answer. Do you have parents?"

"My dad left when I was five. He lives up in Yorkshire with his latest wife, number four, I think. He's not someone who ever showed interest in my life. My mum did all the hard work."

"And what is her reaction to your 'situation'?"

"You mean, does she know I'm a prostitute? What do you think?"

"She doesn't know. Does she know anything about your life?"

"All she knows is that I live here," Tate flushed red, "and we have a housekeeper. Oh, and Bill is called Richard."

"So, Tate's Mum..."

"Eileen, her name is Eileen."

"So, Eileen thinks her girl is safe, happy and living her dream. I suppose she sleeps better than she would knowing the truth, so I see why you've lied. From my experience though, any life built on lies cannot last. Eventually people get hurt. I mean have you looked in the mirror recently. What would your mum feel if she saw you, the state you're in?"

Tate swallowed hard. The scenario with her mum, had played over in her head a thousand times, but she would not tell her. She could not risk her Mum's entanglement in Bill's seedy world, besides where would she begin, when so many lies had already been told.

"What would your mum advise you to do, if she knew your real situation?"

Tate knew what her mum would do. She would have a plane ticket ready for the same day and fly her home, to safety. "That doesn't mean it's the right thing for ME. She has no idea how sensitive and caring Bill is capable of being, and what protection he offers."

"Where was your protection, when this happened Tate?" Maria waved her hand towards her.

"He has to work. He can't be around me twenty-four seven." She almost believed the words as she defended his name.

"You are a *good* girl. You should never have fallen into all of this. You still have time, to start a new chapter, away from here. I have a little money and could help you, enough to get you on a plane, home."

"I am home, this is my home."

"No. This is just a house. Nothing about this place is a home, Tate."

Tate walked around the table to where Maria now stood and hugged her as tight as her pain would allow, "Thank you, for everything you have done already. You are so kind and lovely but please, please don't worry about me. I really do have this under control. I plan to help Bill start a new life with me, get him away from all this too…"

Maria pulled away, kissed Tate's hand and walked towards the kitchen, "This washing won't do itself you know. I have much to do."

Tate watched Maria expertly move around Bill's kitchen before returning to her seat and turned her face back to the sun, as her latest delivery of flowers arrived at the gate.

The flower delivery van arrived every other day. Claudia, the cheerful florist would pop her head around the door, "How is the patient today?" Nevertheless, even she was on the payroll of Paul, a friend of his wife who he helped set up in business, no doubt for money laundering purposes. The pampering was a treat though, and he even arranged for a beautician to tidy her eyebrows and nails, who promised to come back when her wounds healed for skin treatments. Maria greeted Claudia, who got to work on dotting the fresh flowers around the villa.

"Great to see you up and about! You are looking stronger today." Claudia shouted over as she climbed back into her van. Tate waved and gave a 'thumbs up' in response. The flowers were flattering but needed to stop now, she would ask Bill when she eventually got to see him again.

Since the 'accident' and her relegation to Bill's spare room, he was busy and out most of the time. With only Maria for company, (Bill forbade her friends to visit,) her happiest moments were her daily chats on the phone with Irena who was her window to the outside world.

Irena – her first friend on arriving in the town and from the moment she wandered into her little shop, she knew they would get along. Irena wore those low crutched baggy trousers. The ones which reminded her of Aladdin, and although they were not Tate's style, she could not deny how cool and comfortable they were. Irena always teamed them with a tight-fitting vest and half an arm full of bracelets. Her hair hung loose down her back in curls, and she only ever wore mascara and Vaseline for her lips. A pretty, hippy chick. Her warmth drew people to her, and Tate was no exception.

A rainbow of scarves and sarongs hung from the ceiling of her shop, together with crystals and chimes. Incense permeated the air and the ambient backtrack was hypnotic. Trinkets and gifts covered every surface, which Irena lovingly wrapped with tissue for each customer. The shop remained cool even in the hottest part of the day and often people dropped in for a chat and iced tea.

Tate missed six of Irena's calls before she managed to speak to her and explain what happened. Irena was desperate to call over and check her friend was ok, see with her own eyes, but Tate pleaded with her to stay away. Instead, they agreed to chat every day until Tate was well enough to visit Bazaar.

Irena was suspicious of Bill. She knew his reputation for being untrustworthy, his attitude towards women and tried to steer Tate away. However, it was too late because she fell prey to his big brown eyes, which made her feel like she was the only one they looked at that way. If only it had been true, if only he really did save those looks for her alone.

Tate popped her medication into her mouth and swallowed it with her freshly squeezed orange juice. She hoped it would aid her throbbing head.

Bill ran up the driveway and around onto the terrace, "Hey. How are you this morning?" Bill's t-shirt was sweat-soaked, and he peeled it off and wiped his torso, "only managed three miles before it got too hot."

Her heart raced and she self-consciously fiddled with her hair, which needed washing.   His taut chest had a slight covering of silver hair and his lone tattoo sat high on his right bicep. It was a simple design, just the name Ellie, and the date she was born. On the day she was born he went out to wet the baby's head and came home with a tattoo. Juliet, his wife, lay struggling in hospital after an emergency caesarean whilst he was out on the lash. Nevertheless, he was only twenty-three at the time and knew nothing about how to be a good husband or father. Sometimes she wondered whether he had learnt anything in the eighteen years that followed.

 "A little better." She lent her head to the side and pressed her still swollen lip with the tips of her finger. It did not hurt to touch, and the swelling was subsiding.

"Good to see you up and about," Bill touched her shoulder as he passed and dived into the pool. She longed for his touch and to be kissed by him, but his mind was already somewhere far from her.

"I didn't see you leave for your run."

"Needed to clear my head."

He disappeared back under water, and she watched as he confidently swam lengths of the pool, he was in good shape. "Can I sleep in your room again now I'm up and about? I'm lonely all by myself."

"Huh?" He pushed his wet hair away from his face.

"Can I sleep in your room again? I feel much better."

"I don't think that's a good idea. I don't want to disturb you with the hours I keep. Best you get the rest you need and make a full recovery. You know, you're still fragile." He smiled and swam a length of the pool underwater.

Tears stung her eyes beneath her shades. She stood up and turned away, it was time for her to take a shower and make an effort, why would he want her, when she looked such a mess? She needed to up her own game if she was going to recapture his attention.

Her mobile rang- it was Irena. "Hey you. One moment, I'm just heading to my room for a rest." Tate collapsed onto her crisp white sheets and attempted to sound chirpy. Irena was always looking for reasons to slag Bill off, and she was not about to give her any.

"How is the patient today? Just say when you are ready, and I can pick you up. You can spend a morning with me here at the shop. I will give you a crash course in yoga and wrapping gifts in the shop. You can be the iced tea girl, as in you make them and I drink them..."

Tate laughed, the first time since the attack. It felt good. "Do you know what? I'd like that, but I will ask Maria to drop me in town. How about tomorrow morning? Say, 10?"

"Perfecto. Ten is when I officially open anyway. Okay let's catch up properly tomorrow, can't wait. See you then. Adios, Hasta Luego."

Tate felt a flutter of excitement in her tummy, suddenly engulfed by the oppression of his villa - she longed to leave the cold, clinical interior and feel the warmth of Irena's cosy shop. Bill popped his head around the door, dry apart from his slightly dripping hair that ran down his stubbly face.

"Who was that on your phone?"

"Oh no-one. Just Irena." She sat up as straight as her bruises would allow and crossed her legs. Her mobile needed charging.

"And?"

"And what? She was just asking if I felt up to a visit at the shop tomorrow. I do, but don't worry I refused her offer of a lift. Thought I would ask Maria."

"Are you sure you're up to it? I mean, you still look dreadful."

She turned away.

"I didn't mean it in that way. I meant you just still look so fragile." He sat on the bed next to her. She pulled her legs into her chest and winced. "See what I mean."

She sighed. She could not work him out. It felt like this was genuine concern, but she knew what a good actor he was. She had seen it with her own eyes on many occasions around Paul and Tony. Pretending to be someone he wasn't.

"I really need to get out Bill. I haven't left here since…well since… *that day*," her voice broke and she cleared her throat, "and I am beginning to feel a bit hemmed in."

"Sure. I didn't think," he tucked a strand of hair behind her ear. "Okay but I will drop you as close to the door as my car will allow. And if I am not around when you want to leave, I will arrange for you to be collected."

A smile crept to her face, as her eyes reached deep into his. She only ever wanted him to love her. The way she felt right now, was what kept her near him, the reason why she could not let him go. It felt like there was only her, like he genuinely cared.

"Bill," she closed her eyes and leaned in to kiss him full on the lips.

 He pulled back, "No, it's too soon."

"Bill, I want to, I *need* this."

She kissed him again, confident that he would give in as she lifted his hand to her breast.

"You poor, poor thing," he whispered in her ear as he laid her back gently on the bed. He trailed his lips tenderly across each bruise on her battered body. Every kiss healed her a little more and she savoured his gentleness. As their kiss deepened, she knew for this moment at least, he was hers again.

Bill

Bill pulled up the narrow street, parked as close to 'Bazaar' as he could, and ran around to help Tate out of the car. He did not go inside the shop, where Irena was busy displaying items just by the doorway. They never got on, as she was not someone he understood. If he was being honest, she was not the type of women his charm worked on and that left him feeling uneasy, so he always gave her a wide berth. He remembered a time when Tony was collecting protection money, from local businesses. She stood up to him and refused to pay him a penny. She must have caught him on a good day because Tony was so impressed by her gutsy attitude that he left her alone and ensured that no one else touched her either. She was a tough cookie.

"Call me when you need to get back. Okay?" Bill kissed Tate's cheek and nodded to Irena who reciprocated with a half-hearted head flick before he drove away. His mind switched. He had a huge problem to figure out. How the hell, was he going to get out of the drug trafficking dilemma, when 'No' was not an option? Images of Celia in the sauna clouded his business mind and he struggled to focus. He still had some time and as long as he made the right noises, it would all work out.

He snaked along the mountain roads, just as the dark clouds, which loomed with the promise of rain all morning, broke. His windscreen wipers eagerly sprung into motion, swishing away the rare sploshes of precious rain. He imagined a cheer echo around the mountains, as the dusty soil gratefully sucked up the offering. It was, as always, short lived - not even enough to notice unless you stood out in it. Rain in these parts was as rare as seeing the sun on holiday in the UK.

One of his favourite childhood memories was caravanning in Wales. The excitement built for the weeks leading up to their two-week breaks. He was only six on his first holiday and Wales felt as far as America back then, to him anyway.

The caravan belonged to an Aunt and was her pride and joy with nets at the windows and chintzy wall lights. It was compact, but it did the job and was home for from home. If you craned your neck, you could see the sea from the front window. The fish van would rock up every Friday teatime, and the campers would form an orderly queue for their supper. The smell of salt and vinegar wafted down the line and set tummies grumbling in anticipation. Fish and chips never tasted as good as they did out of the paper in Wales. Life was simple then. His life these days was anything but.

He lit a cigarette and his mind swung to Tate. He had a soft spot for her, but she was becoming a tie. He never meant for her to move in or be anything but a 'bit of fun'. The attack had forced this on him. It was stifling him and preventing him inviting Celia over whenever he wanted. She was classy and somehow the idea of renting a room with her felt seedy, well, more so than usual. His guilt witnessing Tate wince in pain, was messing with his head. She took what *he* was owed and nearly paid with her life, and yet there was no malice in her eyes towards him. He knew she was in love with him- it was evident, but he needed to move her out, regain control of his life. Trouble was all the time she sauntered half-naked around his villa he was incapable of keeping his hands off her lean taut frame. But he was feeding her attachment.

The first moment, when she walked into Caminos introduced as one of their 'latest employees', his attraction was evident. She stood out from the others. He tried to have her to himself from the beginning, made it clear she was his favourite. Nevertheless, she was there to do a job, and it was only more recently, he finally managed to bag exclusive rights. She was no prostitute, not really.

One tequila-fuelled night, he set up a session with one of the other girls. But Tate, coolly declined, collected her shades and cigarettes saying over her shoulder "that's not my style."

Paul would have beaten her or worse on that refusal.   She was lucky Bill was not like them, forgetting your place in their world, was risking your life. He tried to explain how it all worked, but Tate was different- she was an actor pretending to be brazen, but he could see through it. He saved her from all the others; he really was her saviour. She should be grateful to him.

He parked up next to Paul's car and stuffed his cigarettes into his pocket along with his keys and mobile. Caminos was empty, apart from the boss.

"Two coffees, "he shouted to Jose, who was busy sweeping and mopping the floor but stopped immediately on Paul's request.

"William. Good morning to you." Paul was clean-shaven and dressed in crisp white shirt and black suit trousers. A black tie lay coiled on the table. His brown hair slicked to the side as if he had stepped out of 1950s Hollywood. Always popular with the women, he looked the part on first meeting, he supposed. However, his reputation was one of brutality. Shock replaced any initial flirty smiles on emerging from a 'private' party with Paul. The girls always got more than they bargained for, and bruising was just the visual evidence. All attempts to subsequently fade from his view were futile, he was only done with them when he said so, what they wanted was irrelevant. To him, they were nothing more than objects in his empire, to use in whatever way he saw fit.

Tate, who had been unlucky enough to spend two evenings in the company of Paul, once confided in Bill, as tears streamed down her face that she was unable to work for three days after each night. He was a depraved monster, she said. This was nothing new to Bill, he was aware of his boss and of what he was capable. One of Gina's lot got too cocky for his liking once. Word got back to Paul that she had sampled a little too much of his 'goods' and whilst enjoying their effects, mouthed off about him. He sent two of his heavies around to collect her and had her brought to him. Paraded around Caminos naked except for a cuffed neck, shackles at the ankles and hands, which initially roused jeers and prods, laughing and leering. Silence fell when he smashed her skull with his iron fist in front of everyone. Paul's dramatic showcase of power served a purpose. If there was any doubt before, he demonstrated that you did not mess with the boss.

Paul basked in his dirty glory and celebrated with champagne, as two of his cronies ditched her body high up in the mountains, where the wilds animals would enjoy a feast and destroy any evidence should someone ever happen across the grim remains.

"You got any ideas yet? What we talked about last week?" Bill offered Paul a cigarette and lit them both. He inhaled and crossed his leg wide.

"The villa is in motion; I got a website design being worked on as we speak and will be ready to take legit bookings within two weeks."

Bill imagined Pauls bleached teeth glowing in ultraviolet lighting and stifled a smile, "You off to a funeral?"

"Yeh, Salves cousin, brain haemorrhage, last week. Shame, nice guy," Paul shook his head and tutted.

It was incredulous that he could show such compassion and yet be void of any emotion taking life from another human being. Jose brought the steaming coffees to the table and replaced the dirtied ashtray with a clean one.

"Yeah, shame. Thanks Jose." Bill offered a smile.

"So?" Paul demanded.

"Yeah, got a few ideas." Bill tapped his head with his fingers as the cigarette twirled smoke into his eyes. He rubbed them and then inhaled before stubbing out the butt.

"Well, get going. There's shit loads to organise, so I need some names and soon. I hope I don't detect reluctance Bill…"

Bill feigned shock, "I told you, it's all up here. I'm working on it." Sweat from his top lip tasted salty as he drank his coffee. These days he wanted to spend less and less time with Paul. Truth be told, he knew he was on borrowed time with him; that it could be his body offered up to the mountains before long. Paul grew shadier by the day. Maybe Bill was only just opening his eyes to the reality of his gloomy world. If only he had paid attention to his wife all those years ago. She saw their world for what it really was - a dirty one, and she would die before allowing her child to grow up in. The money and glamour failed to impress her, but she wasn't high on drugs and Bill's was already cloudy back then. The severity was softened, and any screams of pain got muffled by chemicals seeping into his brain. It was too late now, years down the line, he was on a one-way street, heading for hell.

Right in that moment, sat facing the crazed monster of his boss, he thought that maybe he was already in hell.

Tate

Although the pain relief took the edge off, they provoked messed up dreams so even sleep failed to rescue her from racing thoughts. She awoke exhausted from constant replays of her attack. She rubbed her forehead and gnawed her fingers. The images her dream triggered were twisted memories of old and new - where her assailant was always Paul. Her clammy hands reached beside her for the comforting touch of Bill, but the sheet was cold and empty.

She scanned the dim room. Her knickers and vest lay strewn across the floor along with their wet towels discarded in a heap. Through the crack of the wardrobe door, the colourful patchwork bag Irena sent her back with, sat neatly upon the shelf. It remained empty. "Take this, and when you leave him, you have something pretty to pack your stuff into," Irena had said.

Tate opened the wardrobe door and pulled the bag from the shelf, it smelt of the incense from Bazaar. It was bigger than a handbag; more of a weekend bag and inside was a photograph, of her and Irena. Smiling together, mojitos in hand – Tate could feel the music and laughter ooze from the picture. Written on the back, in loops and swirls: 'don't forget who you are, don't forget your worth.'

She paused for a moment and then placed it back into the bag, shut it in the wardrobe and wrapped a sheet around her naked body.

Like a ghost in the night, she tiptoed to Bill's room and lent against the doorframe. She chewed her fingers as she watched the rise and fall of his chest. The peppered stubble on his chin glistened with the moonlight, which streamed in through the open blind. His hair spilled across his pillow, and she noticed for the first time, that grey hairs like silken threads were beginning to weave their way through his crown. His tattooed arm lay raised above his head and his legs outstretched wide. He was beautiful and her legs carried her towards his bed where she dropped her sheet to the floor and carefully closed the blind.

As she lay down, her mind refused to quieten despite her exhaustion. Conversations with Irena- begging her to leave Bill, to go stay with her. She had a spare room; it would not take much clearing up. She would even help her find a job. She just needed to leave him. Irena made it all sound so easy, 'Just leave him!' The trouble was, he was her addiction and whenever she was not with him, he was always the lurking shadow.

She envied Irena. She had it all: a thriving business, no strings and a steely spine. She never took crap off people and did not fall for the likes of Bill. She enjoyed a string of bronzed surfy types but was not interested in establishing any kind of long-term relationship with them. 'I don't need a man to enjoy my life Tate and nor do you, if only you could be free of Bill...you will never NEVER be happy with him. Deep down, you know this to be true. One day you will open your eyes and see him for what he really is.'

The image of the photograph blinded her, their laughter, happy times. Did she ever truly feel happy with Bill? When did they laugh or joke around? Sometimes all she did was cry and feel on edge. Had they ever shared good times? She bit hard on her lip and her head pounded. Too much to think about, it was all so confusing, and Irena never saw the side of Bill that she did; had never experienced his tenderness. If she had, then she would understand.

Tate shifted silently on to her side, hoping not to wake Bill and risk him sending her back to the spare room like a naughty child. He sleepily rolled over and his arm wrapped around her stomach. She smiled and closed her eyes. This was all she ever wanted, and sleep suddenly reached out and swept her away.

Bill

A shaft of light snuck past the edge of Bill's blind. He stretched his arms wide with a satisfying yawn and wiped the sleep from his eyes. Why was Tate in his bed? She must have crept in again. It was too fucking much; she had her own bed and room. Maria was taking a few, well-earned days off, and Tate was settling in, a little too much. Why was he allowing her to get so comfortable? The curve of her shrouded body gently moved with her breath and his eyes rested on an ugly black bite-mark. Guilt was back and gnawed at his stomach.

It was 5.30am. With Tate still sleeping, he expertly slipped out of bed without disturbing her and tiptoed outside. How many times had he managed that before? Slipping out of crumpled occupied beds, was one of his many tricks, much easier than disturbing the previous night's skirt, and having to converse.

He checked Facebook on his phone for messages from Ellie and grabbed an orange juice and a banana. Perhaps they would rid his stomach of the shame it insisted on carrying. He peeled the banana with his teeth as he signed into his account.

There was one message from Ellie:

Hi Dad,

How about that holiday you promised? Fi and me are desperate for some sun, the weather is crap here. We wouldn't cause you any trouble, I would even pay for my own flights, although we are a bit skint, so...

Well, hoping you might feel generous enough to spoil us a little. Please please please think about it. We will be NO trouble I promise. Say yes Daddy? ▨

Fuck. That was all he needed, more young women to protect. He threw down his banana skin and typed as quickly as his large fingers on a miniscule phone keyboard would allow.

Hey Ellie,

Love hearing from you, although once and a while it would be nice if it was for some other reason than asking for something ▯

Also WHY are you still up at 4 .30 am? I have too much going down here at the moment, let things settle and maybe, MAYBE I will get you out here later in the year. How's the job hunting going?

Love you, Dad x

He hit send and waited for the barrage of abuse. Instead, her little green circle disappeared, and she went off-line. He preferred the abuse to the silence. Ellie was more like him than her mother and this worried him.

He did not use Facebook for more than keeping in touch, and an eye on Ellie, but Tate's name caught his eye, having 'liked' one of Ellie's posts. Why was she doing that? He clicked onto her profile, to see Tate's selfies in various parts of his villa. The posts were popular with her family, who busily commented on how well she was doing for herself, facts which she did not deny. How dare she imply…use his house as if it were her own? Then he thought about the alternative:

Hi everyone back home, I am a prostitute with no money and have just been beaten to within an inch of my life. My car has been repossessed and I am in love with a lowlife who uses me when it suits him, and he isn't busy chasing other women.

Somehow that did not sound so good. To be fair to her, if their roles reversed, he would do the same. He would let her have that one. That was why he hated Facebook; it was full of people's bullshit, pretending to have perfect lives, whilst they crumbled around their ears.

He signed out, put down his phone and headed to the leather recliner, positioned with an uninterrupted mountain view. It was a favourite setting for Tate's selfies according to her Facebook page. He lifted the footrest up and relaxed back, his hands behind his head. As he crossed his feet at the ankles it dawned on him that he had sat in that chair, less than a handful of times, in 5 years. What was the point of all this if he was never able to enjoy it? So many things failed to make sense lately.

Paul's words shouted in his head, "Time's running out, don't let me down, find the girls...."

What the fuck was he going to do about this? Maybe he could do a runner - but go where? One name crept to the front of his head, one young woman, who would gladly assist him in anything... He pushed her name away, too ashamed that this was becoming his Plan A, and wondering if this was the real reason he was allowing her to take so many liberties.

He should carry a warning:

Beware; wolf in sheep's clothing.

He was more devious than even *he* realised and did not know whether to be relieved or disgusted about this fact. She had better move out and soon, or he might involve her in more shit than she ever bargained for. Today was the day. The day he would ask her to leave. It was for her own good.

She needed protection, this time it was from him.

Tate

Tate yawned and sleepily stretched out like a starfish. As she rolled onto her tummy, the lack of pain was liberating, and she inhaled the musky scent of Bill's pillow before hopping into his shower. Her dreamy sleep and unexpected spooning increased her confidence that she was winning him over. With Maria being on leave, she had the perfect opportunity to show him just how much he needed her. She would sort breakfast out as he took his morning swim and fuss around his every need whilst he ate it. She could be everything he desired and to help her cause, she threw her transparent white kaftan over her skimpy white bikini. Bill never could resist her in that.

Tate opened the fridge and took out the eggs, milk, juice and butter. Then laid the table. To her surprise, Bill was not in the pool, he was asleep in her favourite leather armchair. His sleep was peaceful and his face free from the lines, which usually surrounded his eyes. She should let him sleep. As quietly as she could, she cooked breakfast, preparing poached eggs just as he liked them. When the waft of fresh coffee woke him from his sleep, he sidled to the bathroom to pee.

"Nice hair sleepy!" T   ate laughed as he lent in the doorway.

He rubbed his messy hair and half smiled, "someone's been busy, thanks for this," he yawned.

"Come on, sit down here. I'll pour your coffee and juice." Tate pointed to a chair facing the Mediterranean and a clear blue sky. "I'll just plate up your eggs."

"You look better, managing all this too. I'm impressed." He was slowly waking up with the aid of the caffeine, "You not eating too?"

"Oh, I had mine an hour ago! I let you sleep as you looked like you needed it, you really must take better care of yourself."

"I manage. I'm a big boy you know."

Tate flashed him a smile, "Oh I know," she licked her lips and placed his eggs onto the table, swiping a kiss on top of his head.

Bill shifted in his seat in silence. Tate wafted around tidying as he finished a mouthful of eggs. Intentionally he placed his knife and fork onto the table, wiped his mouth with his napkin and swigged his coffee.

"Listen Tate," he pulled out the chair next to his. Tate stopped wiping the bar down and turned to face him. "Now you're feeling better, I really think it's time for me to sort that car out for you and get you settled back home."

The words flew about the ether in front of her, she tried to pull them together, to make sense of them, but her brain could not comprehend what he said. Her face paled.

"You ok?" he patted the chair.

"Me? I'm fine, just a little dizzy." She slumped heavily next to him and rested her weighty head on her arm. Her plan was a failure; he did not need her at all. He wanted her to leave.

"It's just that, I'm not ready to move anyone in permanently, you see. I liked things how they were before, you do understand. Maria will be back in a few days, and she will take care of everything here and you, well, you can just enjoy being my guest again." Bill reached out to touch her arm, but instead lifted up his coffee and sat back in his chair.

Tate gasped for air; her head spun. The truth was that she had no home. Three missed rent payments for her crappy room. She had been convinced he would ask her to move in with him. How had she read this so wrong? Shit. She was now on the streets too.

"Yes, of course. I never expected to stay," she pulled at the skin on her flushed neck. "It's way too soon for all that heavy shit...in fact I'm going to get my stuff together, can you...will you drop me at the shop, once I am packed? Irena and I have already discussed me moving in." She stood up and tucked her hair behind her ears, offering an empty smile. Irena was desperate for Tate to leave Bill. She would love this.

Bill's smile reached all the way to his eyes, "Sure. Let me finish this and take a shower. These eggs are delicious by the way." Tate stood for a moment as Bill restarted his food, and then dragged her weary body to the spare room, leaving him to finish eating.

She pulled her bag from the wardrobe and fought the urge to scream as she threw in her pitiful number of belongings. Was that her entire world packed into that patchwork bag? This was not how she wanted her life to be, she could not go on like this.

She dialled Irena.

"Tate! You ok?" The shop sounded bustling in the background.

"Hey Irena, fancy a house guest for a while?"

"Do you mean it? You've left him? Shall I come get you? I can close up right now! Where are you?"

"No, I haven't left forever, but we have agreed that it's too soon for a permanent arrangement. Time for me to go. Trouble is I have nowhere to *go*."

"Sure you do, my spare room. It's small though, and I'll have to shift some stock to make room. Shall I come over now? I told you, you always have a place here. Oh Tate, this could be such a good thing, you'll see."

Tate fought back the tears threatening to steal her voice, "NO! I mean, no thanks, Bill, well Bill said he will drop me off in about an hour I guess."

"Okay, see you then, Tate? Are you ok?"

Tate ended the call and her delayed sobs echoed around the bathroom. She splashed her face with cold water and stared at her ghostly reflection. How was this happening, what the fuck was going on? She would end up with nothing if she did not get a grip, and sort her life out. If only Bill knew what he was missing out on.

He needed to know what he was pushing away. She glossed her lips and threw her hair up into a high ponytail. Over her bikini bottoms, she pulled on her denim hot pants and slipped her pink converse pumps onto her feet. Her bronzer banished her sallow face, and she threw her empty perfume bottle into the bin after spraying the last of it all over. She closed the wardrobe and checked her appearance in the mirror, surprised at how well she scrubbed up in five minutes.

"Tate? Are you ready? Have you got everything you need?" Bill knocked on the door.

"U-huh, one house guest, ready to go," she opened the door and dragged her bag along the tiled floor. She bent down to adjust her shoe, lingering for longer than necessary, and relished Bill's hungry eyes roaming her body.

"You look ready," he slapped her bottom. She stood up straight and feigned hurt with a stuck-out lip. He leaned in close to her. Was he going to kiss her? Perhaps he would change his mind and carry her off to bed.

He lifted her bag from the floor and gently kissed her cheek. "Where to? Bazaar?" He beamed like a keen taxi driver. He sounded happy to be saying goodbye to her, or perhaps she was just feeling over sensitive.

"Yes, for now until I can get sorted. It will be nice to have another woman around too, not quite ready to be on my own." Perhaps being with Irena would be healing.

"Sounds like a plan, let's go. You still have your key, don't you? So, I can still call you if I need you?" His hand rubbed her bottom.

Tate nodded but the lump in her throat prevented her from speaking a word.

"I'll call you as soon as your car's sorted. It's the least I can do."

Tears rolled down her cheeks, it felt like a business transaction, and she thought they had moved passed this. She wiped her face with her sleeve and instantly regretted it as she stared at the bronzer smear.

"Thanks," said her tiny voice. All she could think about was reaching Irena and downing a bottle of vodka, she just wanted this part over.

BY EARLY MORNING, the air was humid and clung like heavy weights making every movement difficult or maybe it was just her overwhelming despair. Despite Tate's resistance, Irena insisted she unpack immediately, "It will make you settle quicker," her wise friend told her as she sent her upstairs whilst she served the flurry of customers who bustled about her shop speaking German, just before siesta.

"If your German is under par, scoot upstairs now and do it, I need to concentrate, I only have limited vocab." Her smile lit up her face and Tate could not resist doing as instructed.

The spare room was exactly as Irena described. Compact and essentially overflow storage for stock items, but it was clear she had hastily dressed the bed with clean linen and given the room a freshen-up. The shutters were wide open and through the fly screen and bars, Tate could see the mountains over the rooftops. They were the same ones she admired from *his* villa. Tears threatened to blind her, but she wiped them away with a tissue from the chest of drawers and took a deep breath.

With most of the stock items hidden under the bed, only a few cardboard-boxes remained stacked in the corner, but an array of sequined wraps thrown over the top, to disguise them. They reminded Tate of a belly dancers costume and images of Irena's party the previous summer lit up her thoughts. All the girls and even a few of the men adorned the wraps as Irena's cousin instructed everyone how to shake their hips and wiggle to the music. By the time most people were on their eighth cocktail, they did not feel as though instruction was necessary and each seem to find their own groove. Jeff, some friend of Irena's, hopped on top of the table and mimicked the instructor, move for move. His natural ability was brilliant and nailed every detail, but somehow, his bulky frame, chiselled features and beefy arms did not hold the same allure as the delicate female clicking and shaping to the rhythmic music. Tate chuckled, that had been one of her favourite nights. No one knew her and she could have been anyone with any job.

As her hands found places to store the pitiful contents of her life, appreciation towards her friend glowed in her tummy. The room felt both comfortable and comforting, like a giant hug wrapped around her body. Bill's place seemed stark in comparison.

Tate noticed the tiny sink in the corner, and a towel hung next to it. A small basket, filled with toiletries sat on the chest of drawers and she pulled a travel -sized soap from it. The delicate wrapper was floral, and the words promised rejuvenation. She needed that and the desire to freshen up and wipe her day away overwhelmed her. As she ran the cold tap and splashed, it felt like nectar, cooling her pores and cleansing her soul. This was her baptism, her new beginning. She just hoped it would penetrate all the way to her aching heart.

Tate dried off her face and climbed onto the comfortable bed. The rhythmic shop music carried gently upstairs and she as her breathing slowed, she fell asleep.

Irena woke Tate with a cup of herbal tea, "Hey wake up, my work is done for the day and now it's time to go out! Come on, sit up and drink this. We must celebrate your moving in Tate. We will begin with cocktails at eight and work our way to Jo Jo's. I think there may even be music there later. I will call her and book us in for nine-thirty. Now get up and showered...I don't shut the shop early for nothing."

Irena's excitement was contagious, and her siesta had indeed rejuvenated her. But her stomach lurched, and her smile faded. Ashamed, her words failed.

"Tate, what is it?" Irena's head tilted and her lips pursed.

Tate shook her head slowly. She had no money, nothing.

Irena put her hand on her friend's shoulder, "Tomorrow, you will help me in the shop. I have some errands to run and will need to be out. Tonight, is my treat, otherwise I will feel like I am taking liberties with our friendship."

Tate pulled Irena into a firm hug; how many people cared enough to save your pride? Her arms held her tight, and she whispered, "I can never thank you enough for this, all of this..."

"That's just what friends do. You are here, I would rather you be here with me than in his clutches. He will bring you no peace or happiness. Not another word about him tonight, he ruins my mood. Come on get yourself ready! We are going out-out!"

Bill

Bill's steps were light, and he breathed in the silence of his villa. No Maria, No Tate and a mobile full of willing females. He scrolled through the names, but not one stirred him enough to call. He was done with them, for now. Boredom in the bedroom arrived when you realised that there was no thrill in paying someone for their time, he wanted a willing participant, there purely by choice and not because they needed money to eat.

Tate ticked the boxes for this, but the heavy responsibility of her was clouding his fun. He would call her at some point, it was as inevitable as the sun rising. They had something but he could never give her the full commitment that she wanted. Once she settled with Irena, and her clinginess cooled, he would invite her over and they could pick up again, like the old days.   Besides, the memory of her nipples slightly visible through that white bikini and her tight tanned arse, bent over in those hot pants was difficult to forget. How he managed to stop himself from ripping them off was a mystery to him. He was either losing his touch or finally growing up – he could not decide which.

Whilst he thought about her, he emailed sweaty Alan, a podgy car salesman with plastic shoes and ill-fitting suits, to order a midnight blue Fiat, with leather interior. He would also sort out a petrol card for her, so she never had to worry about fuel. Brownie points to the max meant Tate would be grateful, very grateful.   Sweaty Alan owed him for some big business he recently sent his way, so he got a good deal, and the car would arrive complete with giant bow. Tate would love that. She would interpret it as a token of love; forget about leaving his villa. She did not hold grudges, luckily for him. He did not personally need her forgiveness, but if she was going to be part of his next move, it was necessary, and things were panning out that way.

His finger toggled the list of females on his phone and settled on one. Celia. She had texted him twice already which he had not replied to. He wasn't going to seem desperate, "Hey, what you up to?"

"Oh Bill, hi! Thought you had left the country…just sun-bathing."

"You want to sun-bathe at mine? I'm home alone and could do with some female company…although I must warn you, bathing suits are not allowed here…"

"I'm not sure…"

"Huh?" Bill was not used to refusals. His skin prickled and his determination flared. "I'll pick you up in fifteen minutes."

"Ooh, Bill, you're so forceful." Celia giggled and he could tell she was caving in, perhaps she was pissed off that he failed to return her text, "Meet me in the square. It's easier than parking up and walking here." That made sense: the streets were narrow and hard to navigate.

"Ok, I'll see you in fifteen."

"Make it twenty, oh and Bill, swimsuits will be worn at all times. Hasta Luego," she clicked off and Bill's smug smile reached all the way down to his groin, where anticipation kicked in.

Bill brushed his teeth, tousled his hair and thought about her tiny bikini and how long it would take him to rip it off her. He shook the thought from his head and sprayed aftershave over his neck and torso. A shimmer of silver caught his eye; the hair at his temples was beginning to grey. He sighed. "Getting on my boy," but smiled and realised that his looks were not fading. Perhaps he would get better with age, all women like a Clooney, everyone knew that. He slipped on his shades and with keys and mobile, headed for his car.

As he pulled into the side of the square, near to the property place, he wondered if the new 'venture' was listed yet, and decided after his fun with Celia, which he desperately needed, he would call Paul for an update. He would tell Paul that he had someone in mind, to use for the first run, but he was not yet prepared to name them. That should buy him time. It also gave Tate the chance to miss him enough, to want to see him and then be grateful when she did...

His eye caught a glimpse of a leggy, dark woman strolling purposefully towards his car. Her hair scraped back, her oversized sunglasses and enormous handbag screamed, "Look at me." He looked. He could not take his eyes from her. Celia.

She opened the back door, put in her large bag and as she climbed into the front seat. Her smile stunned him. She pushed her glasses on top of her head and he leaned in for a kiss, which she directed to her cheek.

"Bill this is Keira; we were sunbathing when you called. She is very excited about spending the afternoon in your huge pool. Aren't you Keira?"

Keira poked Bill's shoulder and giggled, "Have you got a slide?"

Bills cheeks flushed red. He stifled his anger. He did not want to blow it with Celia. Did she have any idea who she was messing with? She knew exactly what she was doing, what kind of a game was this? He was no day centre for kids.

"No, sorry sweetie. Just a boring old pool I'm afraid. Shall we drop you back home?" Bill asked in a sickly-sweet voice.

"Sorry, I said would look after her...." Celia raised her eyebrows towards him. "You didn't seem to want to take no for an answer and I didn't get a chance to fill you in."

Bill looked at the tot sat in the back of his car. Her damp curly hair was stuck to her face and her legs were so short that they jutted straight out in front of her. She wore a Hello Kitty swimsuit with pink shorts over the top and she sent him a tiny wave with her two hands. In that moment, all he could see was his own Ellie, and he softened. Anyway, there was a chance the kid would need a nap for an hour at some point and he would have Celia all to himself.

"My home, it isn't really geared for kids you know," he warned.

"Oh, don't worry, Keira's a good girl, she won't be any problem, will you honey?"

Keira shook her head and smiled as Bill drove away a little slower than usual, and more cautiously, towards an afternoon with a difference. Even he could not have predicted this turn of events.

Bill stuck to water all afternoon. He would not drive Keira home under the influence of alcohol. He hated people who took risks with children. Shadows of his past mingled with the images of Keira and Celia playing in the pool. Keira was a 'water-baby' swimming whole lengths unaided beneath the water. She was incredible to watch.

Celia's giant handbag served its purpose. Three differing inflatables were pulled from its depths for Bill to inflate and his pool was suddenly all the colours of the rainbow. His chest tightened, he missed so much with Ellie, times like these, where he could have been there watching her play or swim. Now she was an adult, and it was too late. His mind flashed the most recent message before his eyes. Perhaps he would give her a date for later in the year to visit him. Jesus that was the least he could do for her.

Celia and Keira emerged from the pool and Celia wrapped a huge fluffy towel around the little girl, which dragged along the floor until she noticed and lifted it slightly. She passed her a drink of orange juice and her tiny hands struggled to hold it, but Celia automatically took the weight from the bottom, as she allowed the child to manage it almost herself. Celia was a natural with children and Keira obviously adored her.

"You hungry K?" Keira nodded as Celia looked into her bag and pulled out a banana.

"Jeez, what don't you have in that bag?" Bill was genuinely astonished at the items that Celia continued to pull out.

Celia laughed. "You can't just leave the house unprepared with a little one - you need all sorts of things. You have to think ahead and of what their needs are!"

Bill stomach lurched, he was a shit father and his libido fell through the floor. There would be no poolside frolicking this afternoon regardless of whether the little one slept or how hot Celia looked. His inner demons busily taunted him with ghosts from his past. Perhaps those silver streaks at his temples were a sign. His life was shifting and the road he currently rode was a one-way street. The end destination was not a desirable location.

Celia and Keira enjoyed that pool in a way no one from his world ever did. The old party days filled it with naked bodies and drug fuelled sex. However, today's pool fun was as refreshing as the ice-cold water he sipped. Had he temporarily dipped into an alternative reality? Happily spectating, clapping or cheering Keira on, he hungrily soaked up this interlude. His afternoon, the polar opposite of the one he planned, was nutrition for the soul and he even felt a pang of sadness when Celia asked him to take them back. She must have sensed this.

"Don't worry Bill, we can come and play another day," she winked as she exited his car and planted a kiss on his cheek, "Thank you." She whispered, before lifting the sleepy Keira from the backseat and carrying her around the corner. He watched them disappear before turning his car around and heading for Caminos, where he hoped he would find Paul.

Tate

Tate's banging head woke her from her fitful sleep. The Mojitos were toxic at Jo Jo's and her stomach lurched at the thought of them. Beside her bed, lay paracetamol, a glass of water and a box of tissues. On the floor, the plastic bucket was thankfully empty. She reached across for her phone but there were no messages. He had not bothered to text her, but why would he? She was all better now as far as he was concerned. She wanted to text him: **I LOVE YOU, YOU ARSEHOLE**, but she threw down the phone as though it burnt her fingertips. She promised Irena that she would not make contact with Bill. A promise is a promise.

As she stood up her brain pounded against her skull. She threw back two tablets and opened the shutters for some air. The bell on the church tower chimed ten as she padded through to the lounge and stood at the floor length doors overlooking the street, which was bustling with life. Three elderly men, each in a trilby of varying shades of beige, leant on their walking sticks, as they sat on the ancient bench outside the church. Their wrinkled mouths chatted away, just as they always did: watching the world go crazy through their wise old eyes, she surmised. Two plump women in floral pinnies, with harshly brushed hair and folded arms, stood beneath the shade of the lime trees. They compared ailments as they shook their heads and nodded. The street was alive.

A little girl, no more than four years old, stood pointing to a stray dog, which begged her with desperately sad eyes. Her flaky croissant, semi-devoured, swiftly became the breakfast of the hungry and lonely dog. She crouched down to a squat and held out her hand without fear as the dog crawled along on its emaciated tummy to her. Then she simply offered it her breakfast, which it accepted with grateful tenderness.

There were few children of that age, who would happily share their favourite food with a stray dog, and she hoped the little girl would not end up in trouble for giving it away. Where were her parents? She was too young to be out alone. Just as the thought entered her head, a striking woman with tumbling hair and caramel skin, strode over from a table under a parasol and crouched equal with the girl. She leant in and kissed her before pulling her into her arms. Tate imagined that the mother had watched this unfold and was telling her daughter how proud she was. It certainly looked that way, from the body language she could see. How proud she would feel if her child reacted so kindly. She pushed away from the window and headed into the tiny kitchenette to make coffee. One day, she hoped that she and Bill would enjoy moments of pride about their own little tots.

"Irena! I'm here now. Here's your coffee. Why didn't you wake me? I could have been down here earlier." Tate handed the coffee to Irena, who was busily wrapping a figurine of a dog, as carefully as though it were a gift to the Gods. Tate admired that about Irena, it was the smallest of gestures that meant a lot to her.

"Hey sleepy, thanks. Put it there please. Now, this young lady, Keira, has been allowed to choose something from my shop today."

Tate immediately recognised the little girl as she stepped forward, as the 'dog feeder'. Her Mum stood behind her beaming and tucked a strand of hair behind her ear as she lifted her sunglasses on top of her head.

"Oh?" Tate did not let on what she had witnessed in case it sounded weird, like she was spying on them or something.

"Yes. Do you know what this beautiful girl did? Well, her Mum bought her a treat for breakfast today, it was her favourite..."

"Cwassant." The little girl interjected.

"Yes, it was but she felt so sorry for the street dog, that she shared it. Now isn't that kind?"

"Wow, Keira, your Mummy must feel proud of you. I know I would," Tate spoke quietly.

Her mum smiled and handed over a crisp five euro note, "Thank you so much ladies, Keira, don't forget your manners."

"Thank you, lady," her eyes widened as she took the gift-wrapped package and held it tightly in both hands, "bye bye." The chimes in the doorway tinkled as they left the shop and Irena sipped her coffee.

"Hmm, just what I needed, you must be a mind reader. I cancelled my appointments this morning Chicca; I am way too tired to be doing anything other than sitting here and being nice to my customers. Come, grab a cushion, you can join me here."

Tate looked behind the re-covered armchair, which was for sale, and picked up the cushion from the display, before her logic kicked in and she collapsed onto the soft inviting chair instead.

"Good choice! Now, how did you enjoy our night?" Irena clapped her hands.

"Well, it's a bit patchy towards the end…but what I remember was great. Thank you, Irena, seriously I really needed some fun. My life has been grey for so long. Who was that guy…the one with the chest?"

"Ooh you mean Ricky, yes, he did have a rather lovely chest, but it was slightly off-putting that he kept showing it to everyone…" Both girls skilfully avoided coffee spillage as they laughed.

"Yes, I seem to remember him asking me to touch it, his chest I mean, and I think I did at one point! I was wasted….

but I'm pretty sure I ended up just laughing at the absurdity of the request…he loved himself for sure…"

"You know why? You have heard?"

"Huh?" Tate's face screwed up in confusion.

"Gastric band, he had one fitted two years ago and now he is super proud of his body. Whenever he gets drunk, the body comes out…it's like he cannot believe it belongs to him!" Laughter filled the shop and Tate already felt a little more human, but it was not the paracetamol, it was life seeping into her, one moment at a time.

"You certainly captured a heart, that's for sure," Irena sipped at her steaming coffee.

"Me? Don't be daft." Tate shook her head.

"Oh yes! Did you not notice the attention a certain someone showered on you? A certain musician?"

"Mauricio? Nooo! He was just being friendly."

"Tate, he quizzed me for an hour about you. I had to keep requesting songs for him to play, to get him off my back!"

"I must've been more pissed than I realised, didn't pick up on that at all…maybe in another lifetime, I mean who could resist being serenaded by him?"

"Well, you, obviously. I mean he spent the night serenading you in front of the whole bar, and you didn't even notice!"

"Seriously Irena, if people knew, about me, about what I did for a living..."

"We all have pasts Tate, things we are not proud of. But the question is, are you willing to leave yours behind and start a fresh?" Tate sighed. Her head lay back onto the soft high cushion of the armchair. The pulsating music and aroma of incense hypnotised her into a warm safe cocoon, and right at that moment, there was no place she would rather be.

SINCE ARRIVING at Irena's, she had done little more than mooch about the house or shop in the day and party at night. She was exhausted and her head once again hammered from too many tequilas. Mauricio seemed to pop up wherever they went, and Tate was convinced Irena was behind it. He was gorgeous and talented, but it could never work between them, she would need to invent a completely new back-story and just did not have the energy to devote to it.

She lay on her bed and checked Facebook, to see if her Mum had messaged. Nothing, but Bill was online - his name appeared on the side bar, as a chat option. Her brain buzzed. Although Bill had a post-less account, he rarely used Facebook, he must be talking to Ellie. That was the only reason he even had an account he said, to keep track of her. Tate had been brave, once or twice, and liked a few of Ellies pictures. Typical teenager with no privacy settings activated, meant anyone could look at her pictures. Ellie had tagged Bill in a load of pictures. It was clear whom she took after, and she always seemed to be up to something. She had his eyes and colouring, a striking young woman. She knew Bill would hate her having any link with his daughter.

It was hard to think of Bill as a father. Tate never really saw any evidence to indicate he was one, except for the few framed photos dotted around his villa and the contact on Facebook. He kept that side of his life private; perhaps it was in fear of her entanglement in his dodgy world? Tate clicked on Ellie's page.

She scrolled down to 'photos' and scanned through them. Mainly, they consisted of pout poses, drunken silliness and nights out with various people, but intermittently there would be a gem. One of her and Bill, tagged #me&pops or #lovemydad. Seeing him hold a toddler on his hip, point at the camera with *the* smile, the one that reached his eyes, made her chest pound. How gorgeous he looked, in a more unintentional way than his styling these days- sand between the toes, tousled hair and casual clothes. At a guess taken just before entering the seedy world where she happened upon him years later. Back then, his eyes twinkled; his shoulders did not sag beneath the weight of his victims or crimes. He was free, free to be a parent to the little beautiful girl sat on his hip and kissing his face. That was the Bill she wanted, the one she only ever glimpsed for a second here and there in fleeting moments. Maybe he would return, he was just lost and needed someone to love him enough to bring him back. The trouble was, if the precious daughter sharing the snapshot was not enough to keep him happy and straight, maybe there was no hope after all.

Tate signed out and rolled onto her back, her body ached for his touch. His lips on hers. How long she could keep her promise to Irena and stay away from him?

Bill

Bill typed furiously:

Ellie, I already told you that now is not a good time. It's not because I don't want you out here at all. I would LOVE to spend time with you, but that's the point I have no time at the moment. I bet your mother wouldn't be happy to think you are planning to come over here. You know she doesn't want you to. If you leave it a bit

longer, I will contact her and arrange it properly, she is more likely to be supportive if we approach it that way…then you can come on over and enjoy yourself. I will take some time off and we can travel a bit too…

He sighed, as he waited for her return message. Jesus, she had no idea what she would be flying into were she to plan a holiday with him right now. He would not be able to guarantee her safety. She needed to stay put. Her response cut him down:

Ellie: For God's sake Dad. I'm 18 and I don't even need Mummy's blessing to come visit my own father…YES FATHER, altho to be fair you don't exactly play your role too well…the least you can do is give me a holiday…you always have some excuse…

Bill struggled to type as guilt pecked at his fingers. He knew he was a poor excuse of a dad, knowing that she actually thought it too made it even worse.

Bill: I'm sorry…I know I haven't always been there for you….and I DO want you to visit me I promise, it's just not ideal now…it's NOT an excuse…trust me? Please?

Ellie replied with no word, just a row of sad faces. Then her little green light told him she had already signed out and the conversation ended.

Bill inhaled his cigarette. It was shit timing for her to want to visit, everything just needed to calm the fuck down first. He jumped at the footsteps echoing in the hallway, but it was just Maria.

"Hola Maria, you aren't due back until tomorrow?" he spoke in Spanish.

"Si. But I wanted to come and see how Tate is doing? Is she still in bed?" Maria sounded puzzled as she looked around for Tate.

"Err, no she isn't. She's made a great recovery, mainly thanks to you! She's staying with her friend, I – we thought it was for the best."

Maria's face dropped, and she clicked her mouth whilst shaking her head. Bill blushed like a chastised child.

"Silly man. That girl loves you…anyway, I say nothing more…it isn't my business after all. I brought you round some paella, enough for two but you look like you could do with a decent meal so maybe you can manage the lot on your own." She handed over a terracotta dish covered with a tea towel.

"Gracias Maria, you are too good. I'll enjoy this – I know it's your speciality, you're an amazing cook, I don't know what I would do without you." Bill's rule of say little, when on edge, seemed to have escaped him.

"Oh, stop it Bill. You can charm most women but not me. I see through those words you use; the tricks you play. If only you could just be yourself, let people love the real you." She waved her hands in the air and headed back out towards her car. Bill stood holding the paella with a garlic and seafood aroma penetrating his nose and felt like a little lost boy. The rumbles from his empty stomach pushed him towards the kitchen where he retrieved a fork from the drawer and carried his dish, like a prized possession to the outside table. Maria's paella was his favourite and better than any restaurant could attempt. He washed it down with a cold beer until his rumblings silenced. He wished it were that easy to banish the grumblings echoing around his brain.

He was still pissed off with Tony, for the attack on the villa even though he was half expecting something to happen. Pissed off that Paul still refused to back him in a revenge attack. Bill wanted to grip his neck so tight between his fingers, to squash his windpipe and see him fall to the floor gasping his final breaths and begging for mercy. He wondered if the others also felt this way or if it was just him.

Paul and Tony were equally savage, Bill was beginning to think that instead of choosing between them he should have disappeared and started up somewhere far away. It was too late now his place was firmly stated and there was no going back.

Weird to think back to the days when Tony and Paul were friends. No one messed with them. They were a force to be reckoned with. In the prime of youth, their good looks magnetically pulled women towards them. Although they were reputed to be rough in the bedroom, they were tame compared to now. Over the years, cocaine and alcohol decayed their brains to stinking messes, incapable of feeling. Bill saw them as characters from fiction. Tony reminded him of Bill Sykes, a monster bubbling away beneath the surface. He was a ticking time bomb and the reason for Bill's decision to back away. It was only a matter of time before he lost it completely and then who knew what the fall out would be for those surrounding him. Paul seemed the lesser of two evils, although inside he was cold and ruthless, somehow Bill did not feel quite as threatened by him.

The fact that the two men were once friends increased the intensity of their rivalry. Who had the bigger villa or the fastest car? Whose women were more willing or sexy? How loyal are those around them and what are they willing to do under their command? It would almost be laughable if there were not so many causalities along the way. But it was a war of sorts, and weren't there always casualties in war?

Bill considered the final issue, which blew them apart. They always enjoyed rivalry and back then it was seen as playful, although Bill often glimpsed a trace of something deeper in their eyes when engaged in this 'friendly combat'. Paul crossed the line. Tony was living with Faye. Had been for years although they had no kids. He was a monster. She was a stunning woman, a degree and a promising career as a primary school teacher, before becoming embroiled in Tony's seedy underworld, which was in its infancy. She always longed for children of her own. He wooed and whisked her away one summer holiday and she never went back to the UK.   Bill recalled the frequent bruises, which dotted her tiny body. Faye was an expert at covering these marks, a pashmina, high-neck tops, even makeup, but everybody knew what was going on. You would have to be blind not to, and yet she NEVER spoke out about him. Not one word did she utter against him.

One boozy Sunday afternoon, Paul approached Tony about Faye, feigning concern for her injuries. Tony's' screaming was heard from the back of Caminos to outside the front, where the rest of the lads gathered drinking.

'It has shit all to do with anyone else. It's my fucking marriage, MY wife and you should keep the fuck out of it..."

Paul emerged nervously and downed a short before leaving; sweat pouring from his forehead. Tony took hold of a young blonde and left her broken in a corner before going home later that evening. Bill hoped he had purged his ager on the spent blonde, or Faye was in for a brutal few hours. Bill shuddered at the recollection.

Faye found solace in Paul's arms, unbeknownst to anyone else, or so they thought. The more brutal Tony's attacks, the more Faye turned to Paul. However, their secret was short-lived. Photos of them kissing got sent to Tony. He went off his rocker, "I'm done with that fucking whore…have been for some time. But if he thinks he can mess around with what's mine…he's made the biggest mistake of his fucking life."

It took five men to drag Tony off Paul, who he beat within an inch of his life. His scars run deeper than the ones you can see on his face and neck. Faye and Paul escaped to Mauritius to be married in a quiet ceremony once he recovered. Three children and 8 years later, Faye ignores Paul's infidelities, after all he saved her from daily beatings and gave her the children she so desperately wanted. Ironically, Paul never lays a finger on Faye. It is as if she is the only chink in his armour.

Paul and Tony set up 'separate camps'. Bill stayed with Tony initially: you do not touch another man's woman, no matter what. Tony was ecstatic when he chose him over Paul, which surprised him at the time. However, in retrospect, it was just another one up on Paul, nothing to do with him feeling anything towards Bill. Bill worked well for Tony for a while, stayed loyal to him alone. Slowly he watched the monster inside creep out long enough to commit some atrocity before hiding away for a while. Now, Tony was a permanent freak, who would stop at nothing.

Bill stubbed out his cigarette and swigged the last of his beer. He wiped the condensation from his hand onto his shorts. It was risky taking up with Paul...Tony could have killed him for what he did: being a 'turncoat'. Judging by all he witnessed over the years, it would be a lingering and excruciating death. Tony suggested the money and put the choice in Bill's own hands. A clever move, simple. Buying yourself out, but he knew Tony made it too easy. He had something else brewing.

His phone bleeped:

Paul: You got a name for me yet? Who are the lucky first few? If not, I have a couple in mind. But I'd rather use yours first. Time is running out, don't let me down.

Bill: I have someone in mind. Stop fretting, all under control.

Paul: You better, I want a name by tomorrow, don't fuck with me.

Bill rubbed his temples, his head pounded. He rummaged in a drawer and popped two Nurofen. Those alone were not enough; he needed distraction from all the shit swirling around his head. Celia was his first thought. Surely, she could not be babysitting again. What about Tate? They could enjoy some time together for a couple of hours, he needed to tell her about the car delivery anyway…and now Paul was piling on the pressure, he needed to speed up his plan. His fingers were already dialling her number before he his brain had decided.

"Hello Bill."

"Tate?"

"No, she's sleeping. Can I help?"

Bill was not expecting anyone else to answer her phone.

"Oh, can you wake her up please?"

"ERR…That would be NO Bill! Is it really so important what you have to say, that I need to wake her?" The disgust in her voice tainted the conversation. Irena was crossing a line and his face flushed red. He took a deep breath and squashed the angry tirade, which was creeping from brain to mouth. Upsetting Irena would only make this next step with Tate more complicated.

"You know, I don't understand why you have such a problem with me Irena…"

"Cut the crap, will you? Don't speak another word because your bullshit won't work. I won't wake her up, she needs rest, it's only weeks since she was brutally attacked in case you have forgotten. But I will, let her know you called. She can call you back then…"

Bill heard a voice in the background and Irena stopped speaking.

"Hello? HELLO?" He shouted.

"Bill." Tate's sleepy voice spoke into the phone.

"Hey, how you feeling? Rough?" The guilt returned.

"More like the tequila I sank last night; jeez my head is killing me!" Tate laughed and he imagined her rubbing her head.

"Must be the day for headaches, I've got the headache from hell…Listen, do you feel up to coming over?"

"Oh…" her voice trailed off to nothing. He could almost hear the two voices in her head battling one saying yes and the other screaming no.

"It's just I need to go through the paperwork for the car with you…"

"Oh, I see." Bill smiled. He knew that would do the trick. He only needed to get her to the villa away from the beady eye of Irena and then she would be his again, for the afternoon at least.

"Well? Shall I come get you?" She was hesitant but he knew she was desperately fighting any stupid promise Irena would have pressed on her. "Listen, you and I, we're good together, aren't we? What harm can it do? We can spend a couple of hours together here and sort out the car and then I can drop you back…"

"Okay, I'll be ready. See you soon." She clicked off and Bill smiled as he grabbed his shades and keys. At least there would be no game playing, no children in tow or hairy men to stop his fun. Okay, it wasn't Celia, but Tate would do just fine, for now. Tate was about to prove just how much she needed him, if his plan worked.

Tate

Irena's words stung her ears as she climbed into Bill's convertible. He looked hot, his chin carrying stubble and his hair less styled than usual. He smiled, leaned in and gently brushed her lips with his. Citrus aftershave mingled with the smoke from the cigarette he held in his left hand. Her body tingled. It was not all about her new car. He needed a woman, and he called *her*. Not one of the whores he used to employ, HER. That had to count for something, surely.

Irena pleaded with her, not to visit his villa. 'Go for coffee or bring him here, but don't go back there.' Nevertheless, Tate pulled her into a tight hug and rubbed her back, reassuring her that she would be back in no time, and all would be well. It was something she had to do. She needed to sort out the car details after all.

"You look amazing." Bill said and trailed his finger from her knee to her inner thigh and then grabbed her hand and laid it on his groin, "See what you do to me Tate?"

She smiled, but she knew how easy it was to provoke that reaction with Bill and pulled her hand away. She picked up his cigarettes and took one from the pack before lighting it.

"Maria called in earlier, to see how you were doing. She sends you her love. Even brought round some paella for us..."

"Ahh how lovely. I LOVE Maria's paella."

"Yes, about that ...well actually I was really hungry and kind of ate it all..."

Tate threw back her head and laughed at Bill's 'sorry' face, he looked like a naughty schoolchild. She relaxed back into the leather seat and admired his profile. God he was delicious, and she was utterly helpless around him; he cast a spell upon her, rendered her unable to resist him whenever she was in his presence.

 "How's Maria? I'd like to thank her, for everything she did for me."

"She's good but won't be at the house, as she's not back to work until tomorrow. She really only called in to see you and drop off the paella."

"The paella that YOU ATE!" She punched his arm and he pretended it hurt. The wind blew her hair across her face as Bill sped around the winding mountain roads. She knew Bill and something about this cheery persona did not fit. He was on edge. Something was going down; he could not hide it from her. She was an expert on him.

As they turned off the road and pulled up the twisting track towards his villa, Tate shivered. The cacophony of cicadas tortured her ears. Before the attack, her drive up to Bill's pricked her senses, a promise of excitement and unpredictability urged her to drive a little faster and speed up her arrival. Now she wished he would slow down and perhaps even turn the car around. She rubbed the chills away from her arms with her hands and drew a deep breath.

"You ok?"

Tate turned to Bill, shocked at his perception, could he read her thoughts.

"It's just it can't be easy coming back here after …"

"I'm good." She touched his arm and smiled. It would pass, it was just a momentary wobble, with any luck, she would soon be wrapped his arms. He took two cigarettes and lit them together before handing her one.

"Here. Take your time. There's no rush."

The car faced the mountains, and as she inhaled, her eyes followed the flight of a large bird, busy catching the thermals and gliding gracefully through the cloudless sky. What freedom, to soar without constraints, a sensation of weightlessness. Tate gently escaped the confines of the car and stubbed her cigarette under her flip-flop before picking it up to put in the bin. They headed round the back, as Bill had on the day of the attack.

Blurry images flashed into her mind and mocking laughter taunted her ears. She dropped the cigarette butt as her hands flew to her ears. Her knees knocked, and she felt blood drain from her head like a sink emptying of water. Rough hands held her down as sharp teeth sunk into her flesh. Her scream pierced the tranquillity of the mountain air. Strong protective arms now encircled her, guiding her, coaxing her to sit down.

"Shhh, it's okay, you're safe." Bill whispered as he pulled her hands away and encased her within his sturdy frame. He rubbed her back and peppered her head with kisses, as the memories blurred and then faded like phantoms. Sobs replaced the screams and eventually her breathing returned to normal. She wiped her nose with a tissue from the nearby table.

"Shit Bill. That came from nowhere…"

"I'm sorry, I didn't think how it would affect you, you know bringing you back here."

"I'm okay now, really." She closed her eyes and inhaled his citrus scent. How she missed him, the warmth of his bronzed body emanating through his clothes.

"Let's have a drink. I think we need one." Tate nodded and watched him stride towards the fridge. "How about a cocktail? One of my special mojitos?"

She smiled and her head bobbed in excitement, she adored his mojitos and pulled her smooth legs up to her chest whilst he buzzed around the marbled table. His movements were fluid and he oozed confidence as he crushed ice and shook the shaker. He was hamming up the role just for her. Fresh mint tickled her nose as he chopped and bashed before adding it to the mix.

"One Bill special Mojito, "He bowed and spoke in his best Spanish.

"Muchos Gracias Senor," Tate offered. The words were Spanish, but the accent was English. Bill took her hand and kissed it softly before retrieving his own cocktail.

They chinked glasses and sipped on straws.

She beamed and he settled back in his chair.

"You feeling better?"

"Yes." She paused, "thank you."

Tate noticed the hint of a cloud hovering over the mountain top, but it dissipated as quickly as it appeared. Bill's eyes rested on her.

"You know, it's great to have you back here, just like the old days."

Tate's eyes narrowed, "the days before I was beaten to a pulp?"

Bill continued to stare, as though he was carefully considering his next words. Tate suddenly felt uncomfortable. "So, what do I need to know about the car? Isn't that why you invited me over?" She placed her drained Mojito on the side table next to her.

"Sure, I got it all covered and I've arranged for delivery tomorrow, to Irena's. I hope that's ok?"

"I'm confused. Couldn't you have told me that on the phone?"

Bill placed his cocktail on the table and stood up. He took Tate by the hand, gently pulled her to her feet and wrapped his arms around her. "I missed you, I wanted to see you. You and I, we have a history." He kissed her head. "I just wanted you to know that I haven't forgotten about you, you are important to me."

114

Tate's cheeks burned and tears welled, he really had meant what he said when she moved out. It was just too soon for them to live together, but maybe he was actually falling for her? The old 'absence makes the heart grow fonder'? Her mind was steaming forwards like an out-of-control train. Too scared to break the spell, she said nothing, but enjoyed the safety of his arms around her. This was where she wanted to be, forever.

Bill pulled away and guided her back to her chair, "One more drink before I take you back to Irena?"

Tate was shocked, usually any affection led only one way and he had pulled away from her. It was not in a nasty way but controlled. She chewed her cheek and her brow furrowed. Bill smiled and swiped her glass as he skimmed her lips with a kiss and resumed Mojito duties.

"Bill?"

"I know what you're going to say. I just don't want you to think that I only get you round here for sex, that's all."

Tate's stomach leaped. Jesus, this was it. He was falling for her properly. He must be. She stifled a smile and licked her lips.

"You not having another one?" She asked as he handed her drink over and grabbed himself a bottle of water.

"Me? No, one's my limit. Got to drive you back to Irena's."

"Since when did that stop you?"

"Since I realised, I needed to start getting my shit together, that's when. Why should I drive you around half cut? How is that fair on you?"

He must have had some epiphany or something. Perhaps her attack showed him how much she meant to him after all.

"I can't tell you how proud of you I was, after what happened. Not once, did you moan, or insist on going to hospital, or the Police being involved and that takes a brave woman Tate. I just didn't want you to think that it was because I didn't value you...I was in a hole. I couldn't do anything about it. But it almost killed me seeing you in that state. You, you just trusted me, to look after you and see you alright. I will not forget that."

"Bill...I...I..." Tate sipped her Mojito, her words lodged in her throat.

"Shhh. You don't need to say anything. The car. It is thanks, for everything you have done for me. That's why it's so important to me that you accept it."

Tate nodded, her mind was whirling and stomach somersaulting. His words. Never could she have imagined Bill would say anything like that. The future suddenly seemed possible, the image of her mum here at the villa, living with her and Bill, dinner parties on the terrace. Maybe even their own child would be swimming around in the pool. It could all be hers. Theirs. She jumped up from her chair and threw her arms around his neck.

"Oh Bill! Thank you. Thank you. You know that I'm completely yours. Always."

Bill held her tight, "I know. I know."

"Bill, everything I did, I do, is for you. I would do anything for you."

Bill pulled back and grasped her face in his hands. He looked deep into her eyes, "You would?" He kissed her lips gently and took her by the hand. This time, he did not lead her to the bedroom but as promised back to the car. Her knees were jelly as she climbed into his car in disbelief at the transformation of her life. She could never have predicted this, only in her dreams. As the wind swept her hair back and skimmed her face, she felt optimistic – this was her fresh start, the one Irena wanted for her. It was a new beginning.

"Look in the glove compartment," Bill instructed.

She pulled it down and took out an envelope and before she could protest, he spoke again. "Tate, take the money. It's not much, but it is enough to get you by. You cannot live on fresh air and because of me, you have no job. Take it and use it."

For some reason this offer of money felt different to before. It did not feel like he was paying for her services, but like he was trying to look after her. When the car pulled into the square, she lent in towards him and kissed his cheek.

"Thanks."

Bill grinned, "It's only what you deserve."

She looked him in the eyes, brushed her lips over his and tucked the notes into her back pocket, "Speak tomorrow?"

Bill nodded and drove away.

Bill

Bill recalled the events of the previous day and relief washed over him. His afternoon may have been devoid of sex, but it had been a fruitful meeting in the end. He sighed. Tate was in high spirits, and he was to thank for that. He should have phoned Paul and let him know that he had someone in mind for the first run, but despite the contrived events in the villa with Tate, he felt reluctance. He knew she would do it for him. Before he could make the call, his phone rang. It was Paul.

"Hey, Bill. Get yourself to Caminos, now. Got a surprise for you. First two runners have arrived." Before Bill could answer his phone clicked and he sighed with relief. He had thrown Tate a lifeline, for now. Smugness crept across his brow and his eyes widened. Tate was eating out the palm of his hand and now he did not have to shoulder the guilt of recruiting runners. Perhaps things were looking up.

He sparked a cigarette and pulled into the viewpoint, which in his mind marked the halfway point between the town and the bar and was high up in mountain terrain. He perched on the edge of the bench and looked out across the view. He felt like he was Gulliver peering down at a miniature village.

Could he ever get out of this life? How? He was in too deep and no one he knew ever got out alive. He already escaped one mental boss, could he do it again? He stubbed out the butt of his withered cigarette, stood up and climbed over the safety barrier. He peered below at the steep incline. No one would survive going over that edge. He lent forwards, as far as he dared and then a little more. Underfoot a chunk of stone gave way and he slipped. He grabbed the railing to steady himself and adrenaline surged through his veins. He felt alive and jumped back over the barrier, into his car and sped off leaving a trail of dust.

Caminos was so rammed he struggled to park. He found a space further up the hill and as he walked down, the rowdiness of the bar greeted him. God the locals must hate them all. It was only the fear instilled, from Tony and Paul's reputation that allowed the chaotic behaviour. People spilled out onto the pavement, but the vibe was good. Caminos had not felt this way for years, since the days when Tony and Paul enjoyed joint control, and Bill felt excitement at the prospect. Boisterous substance-fuelled nights filled his memory, back in the day it was more than just the 'office' it seemed to have become. It was where everyone wanted to be. Few saw the underside of it, only the unlucky ones, those seeking to earn a buck by bending the law. The girls, the ones who Paul and Tony picked, enjoyed the attention at first but it was short-lived, and before long, they were cheap whores for any one of the group. At the time, they all felt untouchable. Bathed in the glory of the power they possessed.

As he reached the frontage, the hubbub of the crowd drowned out the thud of the music and the air hung heavy with smoke. Umbrellas shaded the pavement and the drinkers beneath. He wondered where the people had come from. Bill pushed through the friendly and surprisingly young crowd. Paul would be in his usual spot, where he now jostled towards. Dodging spilt liquor and over-friendly drunks, he wove through the crowd until he caught Paul's eye, who then stood and nodded, with a smile. Unease crept across Bill. His flesh crawled and despite the unbearable heat from the hundreds of rammed bodies, goose bumps erupted.

Something was wrong. It was only a hunch. It was the way he smiled. He drew nearer and two girls stood with their backs to Bill. He prayed that Paul was not going to push one of them on him. He was not up for that; he preferred his skirt to be at least 25. Paul pointed to Bill and touched the shorter of the two girls on the shoulder, who turned to face Bill. He was now adjacent with the bar and one final push would have put him next to Paul. He glimpsed her face, and his legs shook from beneath him. He steadied himself on the bar as everything swirled around him. Noise echoed in his ears. Why the fuck hadn't he seen this one coming? More importantly, how would he get her out of this? His breathing was too hard and too fast. He clutched his chest. Perhaps this was the part when he died…when it all ended.

"Dad! You're here finally! I've been waiting for you…surprise!"

Tate

To the untrained eye, Irena's kitchen had been ransacked, but Tate continued to theatrically prepare tapas, by using every utensil and implement Irena owned. The delicious smell of sizzling garlic drew Irena upstairs, but her eyes widened at the sight before her.

"Jesus Tate! It smells good but what are you doing?" She slumped on the patch-worked day bed beneath the window and fanned her face with her hand.

"I am cooking you Tapas! Can't you see?"

"You aren't exactly a tidy chef…"

Tate put down the garlic-encrusted knife and looked around her, "Oops, I hadn't noticed what a mess I was making." She picked the knife back up and continued to chop, "Oh well, I can clear it away."

Irena's eyes narrowed as she twiddled her curls around her index finger. "What's going on? Something is."

"Better lay that table soon; tapas is almost ready…"

"It's HIM. You were with him earlier, and now…this mood…I don't like it."

"Irena, you don't like Bill…I understand, but you don't know him like I do…"

"Don't be fooled. You don't know him either, all you know is what he wants you to know of him. He will not give you what you need Tate."

Tate threw a cloth over the rutted table, and proceeded to dot terracotta dishes, bulging with flavours, around. She could not be brought down now everything was falling into place. Maybe it took her attack for him to realise just how much he loved her. Don't they say that good things can come out of bad? This was her silver lining and she had earnt it, with every blow to her body. Faint bruising still covered her body, and her hands shook with every flash back. Even her hair was still patchy in places, but she would pay that price a thousand times over if it meant Bill was finally hers.

"Come on, pour that wine. I don't want to fight with you. You're my best friend and I love you for everything you've done for me. Now sit up here, with your back to the mess I've made." Tate laughed and Irena smiled but it was not sincere.

"Okay, but just tell me...why all..." she waved her hands, "this? This weird mood? It's like you're on another planet. Something's happened."

"Here, take the glass. Cheers. To best friends." Tate sipped the wine and placed it down on the table. "I think Bill is going to marry me."

Irena fought to contain the mouthful of wine, as she choked on the revelation. "Has he asked you?"

"No. But he is going to – I just know it. My new car arrives tomorrow. So, I'm mobile again, and you can't tell me that you buy cars for just anyone?"

Irena lent on her hands and let out a long sigh.

"Besides, he was so different today. He treated me like, well, like somebody who loves someone. He was gentle and didn't even try it on with me. I think he's realised that he's in love with me."

"Don't. You are foolish to think that he loves anyone but himself. He will use you Tate, and then he will cast you aside. He is not a marriage kind of guy. Come on, think about how you met...about the associates he has...and as for the car...guilt and convenience. You took a pounding for him; don't you forget that. It also means that you can be at his beck and call, once you have transport again."

"Come on, let's tuck in...I didn't make that mess for nothing. So how was the shop today...it looked busy when I came back..."

Irena pushed the food around her plate. Their chat was basic and served to cover the silence that lay beneath. Tate made all the right noises, but her mind buzzed with possibilities and the life they would have together.

After they cleared away, Irena soaked in the bath and Tate texted Bill:

Loved seeing you today. Fancy a visit? Car delivery tomorrow and I am super excited. I could pop over?

She wished she could jump in a car and drive straight over to him, but her text prompted no reply. She lent on the iron balcony and watched the buzz of the plaza. A little girl caught her eye; she sat in a chair with her legs dangling. As her mum approached the table, she recognised them as the people who had been in the shop. The mum perched next to her and took off a wide brimmed hat, placed it on the table and pulled her daughter in closer to that table so that she could reach her supper. One day, she would have a daughter with Bill, and they would sit together, enjoying a meal and chatting the evening away. It would be Bill's second chance at fatherhood, and he would relish the opportunity to get it right.

Her phone beeped and her heart skipped. She swiped on to her messages:

Bill: Not a good time, best not come to house. Will contact you soon, enjoy the new car. B

Her heart sank but maybe he would change his mind by tomorrow. He was like that. His world moved so fast that he was unpredictable. Paul was obviously keeping him busy.

"Irena, shall we go for drinks when you finally get out of that bath? I fancy a cocktail or two…" Tate spoke through the door.

Irena appeared wrapped in her towel and smiled. "Sure, I haven't given up hope of convincing you that life doesn't revolve around Bill. Give me ten minutes."

Tate ducked into the bathroom and washed the smell of cooking away. She spritzed her hair and changed into her fitted cotton trousers and a halter neck top. The mirror reflected her still visible bruises and bite marks, so she draped a colourful scarf from the stockpiled in her tiny bedroom, around her shoulders and back.

"Suits you," Irena said as she emerged with damp hair from her bedroom.

"Do you mind? I had to borrow it to cover up a bit."

"No, of course I don't, it's a good idea and the colours liven you up a bit anyway."

"Tonight's on me! And I want you to have this too, towards my food and stuff." Tate laid out E200 on the table, "and please don't say no. I want to pay my way." She could tell by the look on Irena's face that she did not approve of where the money originated.

"I don't want his money; I know how it gets made. Usually costs the blood of someone."

"Please let's not fight. I can't stay here for free and at the moment this is all I have." Her eyes pleaded.

Irena took the money and shoved it into the coffee tin on the shelf, where their grocery money was stored, "Come on then...I hear cocktails calling us."

Tate took her by the hand and squeezed it tight, at the same time she fought back the tears that threatened to run her mascara. They locked up the shop behind them, and deep-down Tate knew that Irena was busy fighting her own demons. That she was keeping quiet about how she really felt, in order to protect Tate and to continue to offer her a safe place to stay. She would never know how much that meant to her. Irena was one in a million and she felt lucky to have her on side.

Bill

Bill drove the girls back to his villa, fighting the urge to vomit. They were squealing and hanging out of the window.

"Stop it, get your head in. It's not safe."

"Oh Dad, stop being so boring, OLAAAAA!"

"If you don't stop, I'll pull over Ellie and you can walk." She sat back in the passenger seat and shook her head.

"Whoa! Is this where we're staying?" Said a voice in the back, "Ellie, you never said it was this amazing."

The gates opened and Bill drove up towards the house. "It's been so long since I came out here...got to hand it to you pa, its lush. We're going to have such a good time!" Ellie clapped and opened the door before the car had even stopped. That girl was uncontrollable. They ran around the back and stopped by the pool.

"OH MY GOD. I'm in heaven," Fi's hand flew to her mouth. Bill followed behind with their luggage.

"You better get these inside..." Splashes as the girls jumped into the pool, drowned out his words. His head pounded and his heart still raced. If only they knew what they had done by accepting Paul's invitation to fly out. The danger they had put themselves in, the danger that HE was now in. The line he was walking was thinner than ever and he could not think straight. He wheeled their cases into the kitchen and through to the hallway. Maria was cleaning the dining room tiled floor.

"Maria, it seems we have guests."

She looked out the window and raised an eyebrow.

"Before you say anything, it's my daughter and her friend; they've surprised me with a visit."

"Is that wise? After what has just happened here?"

Sweat beaded across his face and the colour drained.

"Bill, sit down. I'll fetch you some water."

He slumped into the chair, his head in his hands, as he attempted to block out the squeals from the pool. What the fuck was he going to do now? He could not guard them every second of the day. It was not safe for them. His chest tightened.

"Here drink this and take these pain killers, you look like shit." He rubbed his temples with his fingers.

"Listen, I could move in for a few weeks, keep an eye on them?"

Bill looked into the eyes of the humble woman who stood before him; she would do that for him?

"Thank you, Maria. You don't know what that means."

"By the looks of you, you won't make your next birthday if this all carries on, whatever it is. You don't look good. See a doctor or something eh? I'm going to sort out some food for the girls."

His phone bleeped with a text. It was Tate asking to see him.

He closed his eyes and breathed. He could sort this. After all, he already had someone in mind for the job. He would organise Tate as soon as possible, and get the girls shipped home after a few days in the sun. Everyone would be happy. He would ensure Tate was paid well for the job. She could even start over. Then he could concentrate on Celia. He would take his cash and leave. All would be back as it should be, and he could live a peaceful life by the side of the grateful widow.

Calm replaced panic and he mopped his brow with his t-shirt as the girls skidded in through the door, pooling water where they stood. As if by magic, Maria appeared with fresh towels.

"Girls, while you are here, you will not bring the pool water into the house. There is plenty of room for drying off outside. Once you have dried yourselves off, please use this mop to clear up after yourselves. This may be your dad's house Ellie, but I expect you to treat it with respect." The girls stood open mouthed at the stern housekeeper and headed back outside to dry.

Bill turned around and raised his eyebrows at Maria. He was just as shocked as the girls. He smiled and she winked at him before heading back into the kitchen where something delicious was already simmering on the hob.

Fatigue, and copious amounts of alcohol consumed in Caminos, caught up with the girls after dinner and they slept it off on the sun loungers. Seeing Ellie as a grown woman, here in his villa, where women barely older than she were used for sex, by his lot, turned his stomach. He did not want her anywhere near any of them. Tate's battered body flashed before his eyes. That could have been Ellie. If anyone ever laid a finger on her, he would kill them. No question.

He needed to see Tate, his time was running out and Paul was impatient, doubting him. If he wanted to get the girls off the hook, he needed an alternative. In an ideal world, he would have more time to prepare the ground, reel Tate in, but the game had changed. He picked up his phone and texted her:

BILL: NEED TO SEE YOU SOON. MISS YOU. MEET ME TOMORROW. BY THE CHURCH AT ARCHETA. MIDDAY. CAR SHOULD ARRIVE AT 11.

He would head out there, once Maria had moved her stuff in and settled, the next morning. She would keep an eye on the girls, and he would not have to worry about them at least. It would take all his years of womanising experience to pull this off; after all, his daughter's life was on the line. His phone pinged:

TATE: I MISS YOU SO MUCH. I NEED TO BE WITH YOU BILL TO FEEL YOUR BODY NEXT TO MINE. I'LL BE THERE, YOURS FOREVER T XX

Tate

A pounding headache woke her initially, but her stretched bladder caused her to jump out of bed and run to the loo. She checked her watch; it was 9.30 and she could have done with a few hours more sleep. Once she read Bill's text in the early hours, she found it hard to sleep. He wanted to meet her, at a church. Somehow, Bill and churches just did not fit normally, she could only draw one conclusion; this was IT. He was going to propose. Perhaps this was the church where they would get married and he wanted to mark the beginning of their new life, properly. Her heart raced and her mouth curled up to the sky as she flew into the shower to wash the raucous events, from the previous night, away. Mauricio recently upped his game and was pressing her for a date. He did not seem to want to accept her 'no' for an answer. Bill would probably kill him if he found out, so she really needed Irena to advise him to back off, although she was flattered. He was genuinely a lovely guy and much less complicated than Bill.

Today was the day. Their day and she wanted to look perfect for Bill. She would remember the moment forever.

By the time she emerged dressed and ready, Irena was already downstairs in the shop. Tate checked her message repeatedly to ensure she was not making it all up. She downed a pint of water and popped some headache pills. It was almost time for her car delivery. She checked her hair and makeup one last time, turned sideways in her dress and smoothed it down. It was the right choice; she decided to put on her navy shift, cut straight across from shoulder to shoulder and fitted to the contours of her body perfectly. The colour accentuated her tan, and her blonde hair rested down her back. This was how she dressed before. Before she sold herself for money. "Not now. Don't think about THAT now," she willed the tears away as she marvelled at seeing the woman she once was, staring at her through the mirror.

"Tate! Come down," Irena called up the stairs, "your car is here!" Excitement pushed her down the stairs two at a time and she squeezed passed Irena, who leaned against the wall with her arms folded. A small crowd of onlookers gathered, fascinated it seemed, by the giant satin bow which topped the navy soft-top Fiat. Her hand flew to her mouth. This was the biggest thing ANYONE had ever gifted her, and her head shook in disbelief. And it had a bow on it, like the ones you see in the films. Two men stood with a clip- board, "Tate Martin? Could you sign here please?"

She ran her fingers along the shiny paintwork and marvelled at the leather interior. "Excuse me? Can you sign here please?"

"Oh. Sorry, of course. They held out the clipboard and her shaky fingers gripped the pen hard. Then they handed her the keys and she turned to Irena.

"You see! Can you believe this? This is for me!"

Irena headed back into the shop without uttering a word. The onlookers dispersed and Tate removed the bow and folded it carefully. She placed it on the back seat of the car and her handbag on the passenger seat before heading into the shop.

"Fancy a test drive later?"

"No, sorry, I'm busy." Irena turned to the shelf behind and tidied the items into height order.

"Oh. Well, I'm off out for a bit. I'll see you later though. Maybe you'll change your mind by then."

Irena did not turn around, "Tate? Be careful… and by the way, you look amazing."

Tate smiled and climbed into her beautiful new car. The fresh smell of leather and newness filled the air as she rolled back the roof. With her sunglasses on, she started it up and the engine purred. She had NEVER owned a brand-new car. So, she paused for a moment to enjoy the feeling and took a selfie, which she promptly sent to her family with a big smiley face. Although she took the narrow road through the town slowly, she opened her up on the main road towards Archita; she was driving towards a life changing moment, towards her destiny.

Bill

Bill arrived early and paced the shaded area beside the deserted village church. He had one shot and he had to get it right. By now her car, complete with gift bow, should have been delivered and she would be ecstatic. He left the girls in the capable hands of Maria, who vowed not to let them out of her sight, so now he must play his part. He needed to convince Tate that she could save him. He finished off his water and threw the empty bottle into the car, his chest was still tight - it had not felt right since he first saw his daughter stood next to Paul. A classy blonde, walked towards him. He smiled and turned away. In usual circumstances, he would have given her the come on, but his mind was too chaotic. He felt a hand on his shoulder, "Bill?"

It was Tate, she was the blonde. He steadied himself against the crumbling white wall of the church, "I didn't recognise you. You look amazing." He leaned in and kissed her cheek.

Tate, buoyed with confidence, smiled. "I don't suppose you have ever seen the real me Bill. This is who I am...I didn't realise I had lost myself until I put on this dress this morning, to come here and meet you." She took his hand, "Are you ok? You look terrible."

He led her around the back of the derelict church to a quiet spot beneath an old tree, where a stone bench stood the test of time and they sat, side by side.

"Oh Bill, thank you so much for the car. It is BEAUTIFUL. I've never had a brand-new car and I cannot believe you bought it for me." Bill stared ahead and said nothing. Tate shifted and crossed her legs. "I didn't realise it was a deserted church, where we were to meet."

"No? They built a newer and bigger one next to the school. Thought this would be a quiet and private place to talk." His voice was low, almost a whisper.

Tate smiled, "It's quiet for sure. Is there something up Bill?" Bill dropped his head into his hands and sobbed. Tate gasped, "What? What is it?" She rubbed his back and stroked his hair; his body juddered.

"No-one can see me this way. Can you imagine what they'd do to me?"

Tate chewed her lip, and despite her mouth opening and closing no words escaped.

"I have no-one Tate. No –one in the world who I can turn to…"

"You have me. I told you, you've always got me… and you have Ellie."

"Shit. I shouldn't be here..." he stood up, but Tate pulled him back down.

"What the hell is it? You can tell me. You can tell me anything. Trust me. I would never betray you. Don't you know how much I LOVE YOU?"

Bill put his finger to her lips, "Don't say another word." He took her hand and kissed it. They sat in silence. So far so good.

"Is there anything I can do? Can we get through whatever it is together?"

"It's Ellie."

"Is she okay? Has something happened?"

"She surprised me. Came over. But it was Paul who brought her over."

"Paul?"

"I can't say anymore...if he finds out I'm even talking about this..."

Tate took his face in her hands and glared into his eyes, "You can trust me."

"He wants us to set up young girls, as drug runners."

"Huh? Since when? Not ELLIE? Did she..."

"Yes and no. I mean, he got her over here, to force me into this. Must've sensed my reluctance and decided to play a game…if I don't sort something out, then he will use Ellie and her friend. Tate, can you imagine how it felt when I walked into Caminos and saw her stood there with HIM? I thought I was going to die right there."

"Shit." Tate winced and grabbed his hand. "What are you going to do?"

"I don't know. I've racked by brains and can't work it out. I thought about disappearing, but what about Ellie, she wouldn't co-operate, she's strong-willed and drawn to danger… guessing that's my fault too."

"You can't disappear, what about us?"

Bill shrugged and buried his face into her lap, "I can't do this anymore Tate. I'm at the end. I think they're going to finish me off if I don't sort this. Just know that if I'm found dead, it won't be suicide, no matter how hard they try and make it look like it."

Tate squeezed him tight into her. Neither spoke. He had no more to say; nothing else to offer it was down to her now. She rhythmically stroked his hair with the tips of her fingers.

"I can only think of one thing to say, one suggestion that might work. It could offer us the chance to make the break and get a fresh start, get Ellie off the hook too."

Bill pulled away and screwed up his face, "Any idea is more than what I have right now. I can't see any way out of this mess. Ellie has already fallen for Paul's empty promises and refuses to hear a bad word about him. In her eyes, how can he be bad when he paid to bring her over to me? I can't be honest with her... can you even imagine what her mother would do if she found out the position Ellie has been put in, I mean..."

Tate leaned in and silenced his rambling with a kiss. Then, taking his hands in hers she leaned her forehead against his and whispered, "I could do it in Ellie's place."

"NO FUCKING WAY. Absolutely not. Do you know how dangerous it would be?" He yanked his body away from hers and walked over to the decaying tower of the church. He leaned against the crumbly wall and shook his head before lighting a cigarette. This was working. He just needed to keep it together.

"Paul trusts me, knows me. I'm older, more streetwise. I would do it this once and then we would leave." Tate was next to him again and snatched the cigarette from his fingers before inhaling deeply.

"No Tate. No amount of money is worth the risk; not even what Paul is paying."

"If it would give me enough to start over and leave with you, then I'd do it. But Ellie would have to be packed safely back home for me to consider it…I know Paul and he wouldn't think twice about using her anyway."

"No Tate but thank you. Thank you for caring enough to offer."

She spoke in a low voice, "You really don't understand how I feel about you, you can't do, because if you did, you wouldn't be surprised. Ellie is part of you; I cannot let Paul destroy her life, the way he almost did mine."

Bill looked into her eyes, "I have to get back to Ellie."

"You haven't left her alone at the house?"

"No, Maria is staying there. To help me out…"

"I mean, you can't risk leaving her alone Bill, we can't risk her being attacked." Tate's eyes filled with tears.

Bill kissed her lips, gently. He pushed his forehead against hers, "You're special Tate." He kissed her again, "I'm glad you like the car, but you deserve better."

"I love it; I really do, but Bill? I stand by every word of our conversation, please know that."

"There must be another way." He took her hand and led her towards their cars, parked side by side. She unlocked the car and Bill opened the driver's door for her.

"Now you know why I couldn't see you at the villa. Ellie had only just arrived; all hell was breaking loose. You know I wanted to though, right?"

Tate nodded, "I understand. Text me later, let me know you're okay? I'm worried Bill, I've never seen you this way before."

He leant in and kissed her. Then watched as she drove away.

Propped against his car, he inhaled a lungful of smoke. That was the performance of his life. He would message her later and accept her offer. Then he could meet with Paul and get things moving. Perhaps he could pull this off after all.

Tate

Tate's head spun. If she did this for Bill, it would prove to him how much she loved him. She would save his daughter and he would be eternally grateful. They could leave Spain and start again somewhere safe and far from Paul and Tony. Bill would look after her and help raise their children. She did not care where, as long as they were far from the reach of the others. Irena would probably lock her away if she found out her intentions.

There was no way she would stand silently by and allow it. She did not understand, would never believe that it was her own idea and not Bill's. He was adamant that Tate should not get involved. It was not his doing. Anyway, he had not agreed to it yet…but she was sure he would. After all, what other option was there? They must protect Ellie.

She parked in the main square and headed over to 'Bazaar' via the tiny café down a narrow side street, to grab two pastries.

Vera, the podgy woman behind the counter whistled, "Wow, Tate. I didn't recognise you! You look very chic!"

Tate blushed and pushed her sunglasses from her face onto her hair, "Thanks Vera. Do you have any almond pastries left?"

"Not officially, but as it's you asking and I'm guessing one is destined for Irena…"

Irena was partial to the fresh treats baked by Vera daily. Although they sold out at speed, she would always find one for Irena.

"Yes! How did you guess?" Tate laughed.

"So? What's all this then? You got something important on?" Vera waved her chunky hand towards Tate and then stood with her hand on her hip.

"I haven't worn this dress in a very long time to be honest, but this was me…every day…before I kind of lost myself."

"It suits you. I'm glad you've found yourself again. We all have times when we are unsure who we are and seem to wander blind through days and months."

Vera was the older generation, wiser and intuitive. Suddenly homesick and desperate to see her Mum, Tate pulled down her shades over her glassy eyes.

"Thank you." She handed over two euros and as the money exchanged hands, Vera squeezed her fingers and smiled before turning and heading out into the back of the shop. Tate steadied herself and pushed through the beaded curtain, which hung in the doorway, and out onto the narrow street. It was shady and offered respite from the relentless heat of the sun.

She looked above and lent back against the cool wall, as she smiled at the array of flora reaching out form every terracotta pot nailed to the wall. It was like an oasis, and she wondered how often she had missed these beautiful blossoms. It was indeed as if she had spent the last year with her eyes closed. She inhaled and pushed away from the wall in the direction of the plaza and her friend. Life was about to change for the good, she could feel it. If she could only get that one job done and dusted, she was home and dry.

Irena was on her mobile as Tate crept up behind her. She eased past the wind chimes and perched on the chair. Irena swung around, "How long have you been there? Are you spying?" She winked.

"Only just got here, I stopped to get us these, you fancy coffee?"

She threw down her mobile, "Sure. You watch the shop, I'll get the coffee," she was already up the stairs before her sentence was out. Tate sat behind the counter and the clutter. There were ribbons and tissue paper in various colours for wrapping. Sticky tape, notebooks with as many doodles as words and a traditional Spanish dish with individually wrapped boiled sweets. This was Irena's daytime world, and it was appealing and comfortable. Irena laughed as she arrived laden down the stairs carrying plates, napkins and coffee, "I hope you don't jump into my grave so quickly!"

"I envy you! It really is so lovely in here."

"Yes, it is, and I have you marked as my business partner in the future. Now here - take this coffee. Cheers!" They clinked mugs. "So, how's the new car?"

"OH, it's wonderful! So nice to drive and well…I've never been bought anything like it before."

"So you say. But buying gifts means nothing. Don't fall into the trap of reading into it. Guilt money if you ask me. Guilt for you being beaten," Irena paused, "I mean for the attack. Tate you took what HE deserved. A car doesn't even come close to making that up."

Tate sighed. Irena would never understand the deep level on which she and Bill connected. Irena never saw the vulnerable side to Bill or the side he saved for Ellie. She only ever witnessed the part of him he wanted everyone to believe. The tough villain that you did not mess with. No words her friend could speak would convince her otherwise.   Tate nodded and sipped her coffee, but she no longer wanted the pastry, and left it in the bag on the countertop.

Bill

"Ellie, I have booked your flights home. I spoke to your Mum, and she needs you home Saturday."

Ellie lifted her head from her phone where she was busy updating her social media accounts and scowled. "What?"

"I said that I spoke to your Mum and…"

"I heard what you said. I'm just struggling to make sense of it. I mean, I give you an opportunity to prove what kind of dad you could be to me…I surprise you with a visit, and you are keen to just ship me back without even fucking consulting ME!" She stood on top of the sun lounger, her face scarlet and her finger pointing accusingly. "You fucking poor excuse of a father. Mum was right about everything she ever said about you." Fi wrapped her towel around her and shuffled inside to the safety of the kitchen.

Bill swallowed his anger that fought to escape and bring his wayward daughter back down to earth, he knew it would achieve nothing and anyway the point of all of this was to get her gone, away from Paul and his plans. He would have to take this one and allow her torrent of abuse.

He put his hands up in futile defence and shook his head, "I understand how you must feel but I just cannot allow you to stay Ellie, maybe one day I will be in a position to explain…"

"Save it Father. I understand that you employed some old woman to keep tabs on me so you could continue your life as normal. God forbid I interfere with your love life…no wait! That's the wrong word, you are incapable of love, let's call it a sordid sex life…"

"You are going too far now Ellie…I'm warning you!" Ellie jumped off the lounger and plunged towards her father.

"Oh dear, going to get handy with your fists now are you?" Her accusing finger stabbed at his shoulder.

146

Bill stared at the rising anger, which was morphing his beautiful daughter into a monster. It was like looking into a mirror. He turned away, "Saturday. Flight is at 6.30 am and I'll drive you there."

She darted around to face him once more, and leant in close, "Oh we'll go. And you won't ever have to worry about me coming back either. I'm done with you." Her voice broke with the final syllable, but she coolly turned and headed into the villa.

Maria was as usual, busy sorting out his life and could not have failed to hear the latest outburst.

"Beer?"

"No, thanks. Coffee, double expresso. Jeez, she is one tough cookie."

"Hmm, reminds me of someone I know." She half smiled, "I don't know your reasons, but I am guessing they are pretty serious if you are risking losing her. She will thank you one day maybe?"

"Well, I don't know about that but what I do know is that she needs to be gone from here. Oh, and Maria, I see it too, who she is like. That's the bit that scares me the most."

He headed for the shower; he needed to freshen up before seeing Tate. He decided that after yesterday's triumphant performance, he should see her face to face, to accept her offer. That he must allow her the chance to try to convince him that she should do the running, as though it were her idea and that he would maintain his reluctance initially. He stirred at the thought of her. She looked different when they last met. Classy and confident, like someone he could be serious about, if it was not for their murky shared history. He could not bring her back to the house though, and Irena's was not an option. A hotel room may remind her of how things used to be, when she was just paid help. He could not risk it; he had to make her feel like things had shifted.

With the latest turn of events, Celia had been side-lined. He wondered if she had been snapped up yet. Once upon a time, he could have juggled a string of woman without a thought, now he could barely cope with one. He sighed. This getting old and going soft lark was shit. Still, after Saturday he could give Celia all the attention she deserved. He could breathe a sigh of relief, and all would return to the way it should be, with Ellie far away under the safety of her mum. Ellie was right. Her execution may have been painful, but he was a shit dad. Thank God she was a tough cookie. A positive in the big bad world, where a long-distance father, repeatedly failed to deliver.

Once again, he pulled up at the derelict church. This was safest the safest place for him to play out his act. No one went there now, and it was secluded enough for her to seduce him, which he also predicted. He already decided to resist initially, women love that, when you hold back like a gentleman.

He sat beneath the tree on the stone bench as before, with his lit cigarette, blowing smoke rings into the dry afternoon heat. Despite freshly showering, he left his appearance more rugged than usual, with un-tousled hair and stubble on his face. She would notice and worry immediately.

He heard her car turn in the long drive and halt, followed by a door slam and footsteps following the line of the path and around the corner. He stayed leaning forwards on his hands but looked up. Tate strode towards him with concern creasing her face. She had no make-up on but looked fresh and youthful; sometimes he forgot that she was so much younger than he was. His eyes roamed beneath the safety of his shades, the soft flesh beneath her sheer blouse, masked only by a flimsy camisole, which covered her breasts. Something had shifted with her. Something had changed. This was not the Tate he knew.

"Bill. You look awful!" She sat beside him and took his hands. "Are you ok? I mean Ellie, is she ok?" She lifted his hands to her lips and brushed them across. Her forehead furrowed as she awaited his answer.

"Ellie, she's fine but I have booked her on a flight for Saturday morning early. She doesn't want anything else to do with me. But why would she? I have been a shit father to her Tate, and I cannot tell her why she must leave…" Tears sprung from his eyes, and he lifted his shades onto his forehead.

"You're crying Bill." Tate grabbed her bag and pulled a tissue from it, before wiping away his crocodile tears. "Listen; get her home safe for now. Then once we have sorted out this mess, we can invite her back properly, together, you and me. We will take her out and show her how it can be. She'll forgive you- how could she not?"

"You think?"

"Sure! So, I've been thinking, about what we talked about last time…"

"It's not your problem Tate, this is on my shoulders…you shouldn't need to solve my fuckups."

"Did you listen to ANYTHING I said to you last time? I told you, your problems are mine too, because to see the man you love in obvious pain, is too much to bear especially when you can be a part of the solution."

"I've booked her flights home and have decided I will just take what Paul has in store for me. I cannot be a part of it all. Seeing Ellie, so young and trusting, eager to live it up in the sun…I will not bring girls out here, not for what he has in store."

Tate smiled, "Oh Bill, you've changed. I'm so proud of you, that you are finally seeing the light. It's never too late you know, for us to start again somewhere away from all this mess. You just need to get away from Paul...and I can help you do that." She stood over him and pulled him to his feet, "But he would kill you without a second thought and you are no good to me buried in some shallow mountain grave. I need you Bill...without you I would die."

She leaned in towards him and her mouth was on his, her hands gripped the back of his neck as she pushed him against the side of the crumbling church wall. With each pop of his buttons, he moaned, and responded eagerly, but allowed her to remain in control, this was her moment, and the power was hers. As her tongue slid across his stomach, his back arched away from the church wall. Desecrated ground. This was some kind of blasphemy, but he already knew he would be going to hell and as she laid him down and lifted up her skirt, he knew he needed this as much as she did.

Tate

This was the beginning for them. Tate's smile was irrepressible as she navigated her drive home. She managed to convince a reluctant Bill, that *she* was his answer. Ironically, now *she* was his ticket out of the hell into which his life had descended. If the stakes were lower, she would never have offered, it was the threat of Ellie's entanglement that forced her hand. Now if she managed to pull this off, she stood to gain a future, filled with Bill. His babies, his love and happiness...he would be eternally grateful to her and for once, she would have a little control over him.

It was worth the risk. Paul and Bill would ensure her safety where possible. The last thing Paul would need was this blown wide open on his first run. No, she would be safe; they would both make sure of that, for their own reasons.

The look on Bill's face flashed into her head. His surprise as she seduced him and how their eyes locked as they moved together; it was as though he was reaching into her soul. They had never shared such a connection before, and for the first time Tate was convinced she and Bill were a complete couple.

The disapproving look on Irena's face crept across her mind. She would need to convince her, lie to her: maybe she needed to make a mercy dash home, to explain her sudden trip. If Irena got any idea of what was really going down, she would probably lock her away or worse, end their friendship. Irena was a huge part of her life and not one she wanted to sacrifice. This plan needed guarding.

What a relief Bill managed to book tickets for Ellie to leave. She needed to be away, back in the UK. Tate shuddered at the memory of teeth sinking into her flesh. If Ellie had arrived a month earlier, it could have been her. It would have killed Bill.

Where they would go and live once they finished with Paul. Perhaps Australia? That may prove too far for Ellie, although she could stay with them for months at a time. She may even choose to move permanently, but they had too many bridges to build first. No, somewhere nearer.

Bill would already be organising their new identities, to enable them to travel out of Spain un-detected. They would have to lie low for a while…what would she tell her family? She could spin them some line about trekking in some remote part of the world, with no access to social media. Her doing this one job would secure a small nest egg and Ellie would be safe. Beside Bill would forever be in her debt.

As she drove past the turning for Caminos, she shivered. Times spent there were never good, and she was relieved that she would never have to visit there again. The only decent soul she ever saw in that place was Jose. He had patched her up from many a beating. Such a gentle soul, yet his eyes saw such horrors. Perhaps, when she and Bill settled into their new life, she could send Jose enough money to escape too.

Her brain whirred at a speed beyond her capacity and her hands shook as she gripped the steering wheel.   Her heart race and she pulled over to take two painkillers with a swig of water. There was so much change and possibility on the horizon. She just needed to be brave for two days. She would leave Saturday lunchtime and by Tuesday morning, *it* would be over. This time next week, they could be out of the country and starting a fresh. She rubbed at her knotted neck and inhaled deep breathes. "I can do this."

Through the window, the dust cloud from her abrupt stop settled, and she looked out over the town, built into the side of a national park. The sun, sat high in the cloudless sky, the perfect canvas for the picturesque, whitewashed houses. Saying goodbye to the area would be bittersweet. She experienced some of her darkest and most desperate times beneath the picture-perfect façade of the view, but she had also absorbed the kindness and warmth of the locals. She wondered where she belonged before she realised, wherever Bill was. That was where she truly belonged.

Bill

Ellie had not budged in her defiance, and not uttered a single word since their argument. He had to hand it to her -she was a force to be reckoned with. Maria ensured they were packed and ready for the morning. He strained to listen to the conversation between the two young girls as they sat in his Jacuzzi.

"You know...you shouldn't cut him off completely..." Bill was surprised at Fi sticking up for him. "I mean, we could spend loads of holidays here, once he has sorted out whatever his shit is..." That was more like it, an opportunist rather than bridge-builder.

"Have you forgotten already? He didn't even pay for us to get out here! He won't let us back. He's an arsehole."

"Yer, well, he's got more to offer than my dad. Just don't cut him off completely...besides he's pretty hot for a dad."

"You're sick in the head. Did you really just say that- he is hot? Jeez, you need to sort yourself out."

Bill stifled a chuckle as he watched his daughter dive expertly into the deep end and swim away in disgust. Perhaps Tate was right and there was some hope for them in the future; that one-day Ellie would forgive and allow some kind of relationship with her. For now, it must be this way. Her safety was his highest priority.

Tate was his sacrificial lamb, and he flinched as he recalled opening his eyes during their sex at the church and the devotion offered in hers. Perhaps their unholy act on sacred land had cursed him, awoken his conscience and dulled his aching groin. Her trusting eyes, so full of love…but still, she would end up with more money than she could have made in a year, he would make sure of that.

"Girls, you going to come and eat? I made my famous paella, your dad's favourite Ellie!"

"In a bit," Ellie responded.

"No, now. Out and get dried, when someone makes a special effort – the least you can do is be gracious enough to seem appreciative." Maria was not someone you said no to.

"Thank you, Maria," Fi offered and immediately exited the pool.

Ellie swam to the end and then back again, in a composed breaststroke. It was her way of having the last word and Maria and Bill shared a smirk before sitting down.

Maria poured the champagne and once Ellie sat at the table Bill lifted his glass.

"To my daughter, whom I hope will visit again at a more appropriate time." Ellie huffed and sipped from her glass. "And to Maria, who looks after us all so well, and for making my favourite meal tonight."

"Thank you, now ladies, let me dish you up some. Do you like paella Fi?"

"I'll try it, I've never had it before, and this is my first time abroad."

"Well, see how you get on, but I promise that I have never met anyone yet, who doesn't like my speciality." Maria scooped the paella onto their plates and then lastly her own.   Fi tasted the very tip off her fork and scrunched up her face, but by the third fork enthusiastically scooped it into her open mouth.

"Maria, this is lush!" Fi managed in between forks-full, and Maria responded with spooning more onto her plate.

"It's ok. Had better." Ellie pushed the food around her plate, then dropped her fork and swigged at her champagne. Maria stifled Bill's urge to chastise her by covering his hand with her own and a discreet shake of the head.

"Well maybe you are the first to not enjoy it. That's ok…paella is not for everyone, it's usually for the more adventurous with food."

Ellie pulled her sunglasses over her eyes and sat back in the chair. She avoided watching Fi, who was happily tucking into her meal and champagne, instead looked over towards to mountainous horizon, chewing her cheek.

"Thank you for having me stay, it is beautiful here and lovely to meet you after hearing so much about you." A harsh thud under the table signalled Fi to say no more. Perhaps he was not the forgotten father after all, and he supressed a smile.

"Thank you. You must come back again when things have settled here. I will book you both flights and you can stay as long as you wish." Fi beamed and Ellie picked up her fork and began to eat.

Later in the evening, when the pool was quiet and the girls sleeping stretched out on their parallel sun loungers, Bill smiled as he recalled the pact the girls had made to stay up drinking all night until it was time to leave. They both made it to 1am, before the heaviness of sleep hushed them. Tomorrow they would be gone and in an odd way, he would miss their noise and youthful enthusiasm for life.

He downed his vodka, and poured another, Maria was driving them to the airport in a few hours and then he would be facing Tate, and the impending trial run. Tate would be the first and last, he would recruit. Once the trial was out of the way, he would ensure that Tony, got wind of their new operation. He would be unable to resist revenge…that would be the end of it. He just had to get Tate through this first. He felt wired and despite the vodka, sleep did not rescue him. He picked up his mobile and texted Tate, whom he knew would be awake mulling over the day ahead.

BILL: CAN NEVER REPAY YOU ENOUGH FOR WHAT YOU DO FOR MY DAUGHTER. YOU ARE SPECIAL AND I WILL NEVER FORGET IT. Xx

In what felt like a millisecond, his phone buzzed:

TATE: YOU CAN REPAY ME BY BEING BY MY SIDE FOR THE REST OF MY DAYS – LOVE YOU BILL xx

Bill sighed.   She really believed that they would be a couple. At least she would have her pay out to fall back on and he could make sure that she never had to plummet to the lows of prostitution again. It was the least he could do after all.

Tate

Tate's dry throat threatened to close, and after an hour of wriggling, she got up and padded to the kitchen. She took an ice -cold water from the fridge and sat on the seat by the window. The square was silent, and the only sign of life were the stray dogs searching for food. Irena cooked a feast for her friend, amidst concerned comments about the trip Tate had sprung on her. Irena was intuitive and sensed her rising tension, but Tate hoped it was genuine and that she had not somehow discovered her secret. Lying to her was not something that she relished, and she hoped that Irena mistook Tate's lack of eye contact as anxiety for her 'sick gran', whom she would rush to visit at a Portsmouth hospital.

Tate found it impossible to convince Irena that she did not need a lift to the airport because Bill was already dropping off Ellie, so she could catch a lift with them. However, this caused raised eyebrows of suspicion. The last thing she wanted was any unnecessary worry for her, in a few days this would all be behind her, and Irena would be non-the-wiser. The large sum of cash could be explained by the 'loss' of her granny, an inheritance and it would be obvious that she and Bill would need to leave if they wanted a fresh start.

The clock on the tower chimed six and slowly the square returned to life…one person at a time. The shady bench was empty; too early for the three old men to sit and while the day away, but shutters began to open, and the bread and bottled water deliveries were starting.

Tate's stomach churned with the sudden reality of what she had agreed to. This first run was a trial for the line. They clarified that she did not need to swallow the drugs, they would have them stitched into a designer suitcase, and after travelling to the coast, she would meet up with her contact who would swap her case with his loaded one and take them on to the next leg of the journey, over to Gibraltar.

What if her contact was being watched or if they were caught? Sweat beads from across her forehead dripped slowly down her nose onto her upper lip. Up until now, she had focussed purely on the goal, her new life with Bill. Now, she could no longer ignore what she was about to do, how she could end up in prison.

It was not too late. She could pull out, run away. Bill had looked deep into her eyes during their recent lovemaking, and he needed her help. She knew what she must do.

They were to meet back at the church at noon, where Bill would be waiting to give her last minute instructions, booking details and her suitcase. He would take her car to his villa and return later for his. From there, an associate taxi driver, would collect her and drop her at the nearest train station. Then she was on her own.

Her throat burned and she ran in to the toilet and vomited. She slumped onto the floor, her back against the bath and stifled her sobs. Her palms smacked her forehead repeatedly and on hearing Irena stir, she switched on the shower and stood beneath the cool jets until her body shivered.

Her instructions were to look like an executive going away for a meeting. Her shift dress was ready, and her shoes polished. A knock at the bathroom door followed by Irena standing in the doorway caused Tate to turn of the shower and wrap herself in a towel.

"What? WHAT IS IT?"

"Here put this on," Irena handed her a silk kimono and left
the room. Tate rubbed her body dry and wrapped her
dripping hair in a towel. The scarlet silk clung to her damp
skin. She hurried out of the bathroom to where Irena sat
at the table.

"Irena what's going on? I haven't got long before I need to
leave…you know that…"

"Tate! Stop! Will you please just stop."

Tate sucked in her breath…she knows…but how?

"We both know your Granny isn't sick."

"Yes, she is. She's on her deathbed, that's why I have to…"

"WILL YOU STOP NOW?" Her hands flew high in the air and
curled into fists. "I know, I mean I don't know where
you're going or what the hell you are about to do,
although I do know if it involves Bill and you are lying to
me, then it must be bad news."

Tate sunk into the chair, "What are you talking about? And
why the hell are you always slating Bill? Bill loves me, it's
not like it used to be…he takes care of me now, he wants
us to be together…"

Irena stared blankly and shook her head. She reached out
to hold Tate's hand, but Tate pulled away. "You don't

know anything and now you're calling me a liar too? Really?"

"There is only one liar in this room, and it isn't me. I thought that we were friends, real friends Tate. I brought you into my home, we were like sisters." Irena pulled her hair back off her face and stared into Tate's eyes.

"We are like sisters! I love you like my own sister!"

"No, you lie." Silence.

Bill's voice spoke in Tate's head, 'say nothing, she knows nothing. She doesn't understand that's all.'

"I messaged your mum Tate. Told her I was concerned for you and that I was also sorry to hear about your grandmother."

Tate gasped and her hand flew to cover her open mouth. She stood and the chair flung behind her and crashed backwards to the floor.

"Listen to me, I know you have no grandmother, so what the hell is going on?"

Tate ran to the window; her hands gipped her knees and she struggled to catch her breath. It was all unravelling. It should not happen this way...what could she say that would satisfy Irena without blowing it all?

"Bill and I, we, I mean we are eloping..." It was the only thing she could think of, that just might work.

Irena turned away and steadily walked to her sideboard. Slowly she opened the top drawer and sighed as she pulled out a large envelope. "Well, before you get too carried away with his empty promises, I think you had better take a look at this."

Tate turned away from the bustling square. On the table, a large manila envelope sat with the seal already open. On the front, in capitals was her name. Her eyes narrowed, and then panic rose from the pit of her stomach, what if it was something to do with the arrangements? What did she know?

"You'd better sit back down; you're not going to like this."

Tate picked up the chair and sat down as instructed. She reached across to pick up the envelope and Irena caught her hand, "You have to know that I only opened it because I was so worried for you. I had no idea what it contained and for the record, I'm sorry."

She pulled her hand away. Tate lifted the envelope, which felt as though it would burn her fingers. Half of her wanted to rip it open and the other half wanted to tear it to shreds.

Her fingers reached inside and pulled out four large black and white photographs, each containing a small digital date and time of capture in the bottom left-hand corner. On contact, she threw them across the table and onto the rug out of her sight.

"No. No. No. NO!" She shook and her wide eyes blinked away the images that now burned into her memory.

"You must look at them." Irena stooped and picked them off the floor, "Look at them!"

"NO! He wouldn't do that to me!"

"Look, here…he is doing this to you!" Irena's accusing finger stabbed at the images. One of Bill with a beautiful woman against a wall. The second of them sat enjoying drinks at the Terrace restaurant. She was drinking in every word he was saying. He looked desperate for her; Tate would recognise that look anywhere. The third showed an intimate moment in a spa swimming pool. But the fourth sent a screaming noise, which Tate soon realised escaped from her own mouth. It was the same woman again but with a little girl, swimming in his pool. Bill cheering the little one on from the side…in HIS pool.

Her dream was to see their kids splashing around with him on the side, doting. And all that time, he was busy doing all of this behind her back.

Irena pulled Tate to her feet and in close, tight. Shock gripped her body; her teeth chattered.   "Drink this." Irena passed Tate a straight whiskey and poured herself one. "Drink it, go on sip it. That's it, good girl."

She picked up the photographs again, "Oh shit! I've met them, the lady and the little girl – she came into your shop!" Her eyes darkened.

"Yes. I remember."

"How fucking dare he?" The words escaped through her tightly clenched jaw.

Irena smiled. Tate's fire ignited.

"How did you get these? I mean did you know all along?" She scattered the pictures across the table and stormed to the window.

"No! Of course not. I could never keep something like this from you!" She reached out and pulled Tate's shoulder back. Face to face, Irena's eyes pleaded with her friend. Tate closed hers tight, she wanted to shut out the world, to stop everything and just have a quiet moment to take in the betrayal. Irena took her hand and kissed it, until she opened them again.

"I know. I know you wouldn't," her voice was a whisper.

"It was an answer to my prayer, it's true. I was failing to make you see the games that *he* plays. He blinded you Tate. He's so convincing at times. But you have never been happy with him, you spend your time scared of losing the ideals you have created, that he has painted for you...none of it was real."

Irena sat down, exhausted, "After contacting your family, I was at a loss, I felt helpless. I knew that nothing I said would change how you viewed him, so last night, I resigned myself to the fact that you would have to go and do whatever it was that you planned. That I would be there for you if you needed me. Then you went for a shower, and I thought I heard someone outside. It couldn't be you, but this had been pushed through the letter box, this envelope. I opened it in fear...I promise, for fear of what you were involved with."

"But who? Tony?"

Irena nodded, "that's what I reckon. Revenge. But Tate, what really churned my stomach is the date on the one of them in the restaurant... look at the date and time."

Tate picked up the picture and studied it hard. Suddenly her brain switched into gear and the date rang an alarming bell in her brain, so loud that her hands flew to her ears, "he was with HER, whilst I was attacked...he was with her..."

Bill

Bill wiped his sweaty brow with the back of his hand and checked his watch again. She was late. He pushed his hair back off his forehead and texted for a second time. If she was driving, she would not be able to reply anyway, but he was sick of just sitting.

BILL: HOPE YOU'RE ON YOUR WAY

He pressed send and then realised it may sound a little abrupt.

BILL: AM WAITING FOR YOU, SO THE REST OF OUR LIFE CAN BEGIN xx

He lit another cigarette and got out of the car. He paced around the church perimeter twice and checked his watch again. It was 12.20. Where was she? She would never back out. Maybe that bitch Irena was keeping her back. He dialled her number, but it went immediately to answerphone. That had never happened before. The tension in his knotted stomach turned into anger. What was she playing at?

Half past twelve. No sign of her and no text, he would wait another five minutes and then he was going to find her.   His phone vibrated in his pocket, and relief flooded him, but his stomach lurched as he saw the caller id: Paul.

"Bill. We all set?"

"Yea. Sure. On our way." Bill hoped this would be true within the hour.

"I think you chose wisely; Tate knows the score- should be able to cope with whatever situation she finds herself in. Remember that I have another two as back up in mind…if this should go wrong, you understand."

The phone went dead, and Bill stifled the urge to launch it against the cracked wall of the empty church. The only good thing in the situation at present was that Ellie and Fi were almost home, and Paul was unaware of this.

At 12.35, Bill jumped back into his car and headed for Irena's. She was not going to get away with this. His neck was on the line now, how dare she screw him over? His car sped around the mountain roads passing beeping and gesticulating locals, disgusted with his recklessness. He pulled into the square and blasted his horn, revving his car, to clear his path. His fists pounded the door or the closed shop until Irena let him in.

"Stop causing a scene Bill and get inside," she closed the door behind him, drew the curtain across and leaned back against it.

Bill's fury rose inside like a rocket with a burning fuse. He stood and stared, his fists balled up tight, knocked against his thighs.

"She's not here, she's gone to see her family. Had a call this morning to say that her grandmother is dying." Lying bitch. Bill did not move. He continued to stare her out. She did not flinch. "Go look for yourself, you won't find her."

He lunged forward and grabbed her the throat. His fingers squeezed her neck and her eyes bulged. As he slammed her against the wall, terracotta pots smashed into mosaic pieces on the ground, which crunched beneath Bill's feet. His fingers twisted into her neck, but Irena maintained eye contact and if she felt scared, her face did not betray her.

"Liar!" Bill raised his free hand and smacked her to the floor, where she landed like a pile of her discarded scarves. He ran up the stairs and flung everything in his path, but there was no sign of her.

"I'll find you. You can't fuck with me," he roared and launched a carved elephant at the gilded mirror, which cracked from top to bottom. Back downstairs, Irena sat on the chair behind her counter. What was it with her? How was she still so in control? He paced towards her and lent in close, close enough to smell the coffee on her breath.

"You've always had your say, chipping away in her ear about me. You know fuck all Irena. Your 'FRIEND' was prepared to risk everything for me. Ask her. Go on; just ask her where she was off to with a suitcase full of coke. I don't think you'll like the answer very much. Once a whore, always a whore." He traced his finger along her cheek until his hand rested in her hair at the nape of her neck.

"Get out Bill," she whispered.

He yanked back her head with a clump of her hair, "Watch out Irena. You think you are infallible, but everyone has their limits." The veins in her neck popped out as her back arched under his power. How was she still expressionless? With his free hand, he pulled open the neckline of her vest top and peeped beneath at her bra-less breasts.

"Well, at least I know that I haven't been missing out all these years. Nothing there worth having." He smiled and allowed her top to ping back to her skin.

Irena laughed, "Is that the best you can do? Fuck off Bill."

He twisted her hair with all his strength and her head rebounded as it ripped from her scalp. Still, her face gave him nothing. He didn't have time for this. He ran his fingers through his wayward hair and unlocked the door. "Pleasure doing business with you," he said as he left the shop.

He lit a cigarette and pulled away, towards the viewing point. He needed time, to plan his next move. Perhaps, he could blame the screw up on Tate backing out…drink a few beers and slag off women in general. Paul would be forgiving, and they would be back on track. Reality was, he would be lucky to get out of this one.

Tate

Tate's phone beeped with a message from Irena, as soon as Bill left Bazaar:

He's gone and he's looking for you. Be quick and be careful.

Tate sprinted to the safe in his office. Shit, what was the number? She punched in a random selection of numbers, but it was no use. Panic rose and she slapped her forehead…her mind flashed Facebook. She whipped her phone from her pocket and scrolled to Ellie's page, where she found her birthday. She keyed in the numbers and the safe opened.

Shakily she emptied the contents into the leather holdall from Bill's wardrobe and left the photograph in its place. The zip stuck as she fought to close it and she caught her finger, which bled. She wiped it onto her dress and ran through the echoing villa, aware of her every footstep. She threw her keys on the table and flinched at the memory of two men towering over her, which fleetingly passed before her eyes. The cumbersome bag slowed her run to a fast walk as she struggled down the drive and for the final time out of the villa - the place where all her future hopes and dreams lay in tatters at the feet of the man she loved.

Tate ran through his gates just before they closed and saw Maria waiting outside her front door, "Quick Tate, in here now!" she pulled her inside the door before shutting and locking it.

"I've put my car in the garage, he will think I am out, he knows I always leave the car on the drive. Irena called, she told me everything." Maria pulled Tate in close, and the holdall dropped to the floor.

"I'm sorry Maria. That I've put you in this position." Her tears pooled into a patch onto the shoulder of Maria's white shirt.

Maria held Tate away from her and looked into her eyes, "Those photographs, how could he do that to you, after you almost died…because of HIM? He was like a son to me, I always hoped that he would come good in the end, but he's not the man I thought he was. It is only right that I help you. You deserve every penny of his money Tate and if you have any sense, you will stay far away. I will not be working for him, even if he does come begging at my door. He is in danger now no doubt."

"Will you take this Maria? As a thank you?" Tate crouched over the bag and pulled a wad of notes, which she offered out to Maria. She shook her head.

"No, thank you. You need it to get as far away as you can. I'll take you back to Irena, for you to say your goodbyes and then you must leave."

173

Maria peeped through the blind of the front window and waited. Tate sat on the bag, which now carried her future and the promise of a better life, on the hallway tiles. She had never been inside Maria's house and noticed it did not echo like Bill's villa. It felt comfortable and was crammed with photographs and personal treasures. The largest framed photograph on the wall was of Maria and her daughter, on her graduation day, when her eyes glistened with secret tears of pride.

"Okay, he's just headed up to the villa, come quickly follow me."

Maria opened the door from the hallway, which led directly into the garage, and they jumped into the car. The engine was running. Maria edged forward before the door was fully up and sped off her drive and down the road, leaving behind a trail of dust.

Bill

Tate's car was parked in the closest spot to the edge of the drive. What was she doing here? It did not make any sense; he knocked his forehead with his fist and stormed around to the terrace, "Tate?"

Her car keys sat on the table. "Tate? You think you can come back here and say you're sorry?" He darted from

174

room to room, but the house was deserted. Money. He needed money to run. He headed to the office and keyed in the safe code, ripping open the door.

"NO – FUCK NO!" It was empty. The only thing left inside, was a photograph. It was of himself and Celia, sat together in the terrace restaurant sharing breakfast. He turned it over, and read the message scrawled on the back:

NAUGHTY BILL & ON THE DAY WHEN POOR TATE WAS ATTACKED. THE TRUTH ALWAYS FINDS US BILL.

A roar erupted from the pit of his stomach, and he punched and kicked at the wall. His bloodied joints left trails of smeared crimson graffiti. His anger spilled in through the hallway, and vases and pictures crashed to the floor as his frenzied rampage exploded. Tony set him up...maybe even Tony and Paul. His imagination fired pictures of them sat in Caminos laughing at his expense. His body lashed out in blind rage, until the contents of his villa resembled a burglary. He pulled a bottle of whiskey from the cupboard and threw the lid to the floor before drinking down the burning liquid.

This was the end. Tony finally brought about his demise, and he still had Paul to face. He swallowed the remains of the bottle and as he stumbled to his car, he lobbed it into the swimming pool. He was not about to wait for them to find him, no fucking way. He could handle Paul; he could handle anyone...bring them all on.

He threw his car into reverse and drove through the barely opened gates towards Caminos. "I'm coming for YOU!" He screamed. "All these years! It's over – IT'S ALL FUCKING OVER!" His bloodied hands reached for his cigarettes and his car sped dangerously close to the edge of the road, but he no longer cared.

Tate

Irena peered window on the door of her closed shop and on their arrival, opened it only slightly as she cautiously peered up and down the street.

"Bye Maria. Thank you for everything you've done for me…"

"Shhh. No time for tears, go now."

Tate leaned forward and kissed Maria on her damp cheek. "It's not tears, it's from the dust."

They smiled and nodded. Tate hauled the bag from the back seat and chewed on her lip, a fruitless attempt to hold back her emotions. Her head whirled and her legs threatened to buckle. Irena grabbed the bag and thrust her into the shop as Maria pulled away. She locked the door behind them.

Tate looked around to the piles of debris, swept into the corner. "What did he do?"

"I'm fine. Nothing I cannot handle. He doesn't scare me. Go get your stuff together NOW. I'll drive you to the airport. You can't risk staying around here."

"What's that on your neck? Did he do that?"

"I said I'm fine," Irena turned away and knelt low to sweep up the mess including clumps of her hair.

"Your head," Tate knelt beside her, "It's bleeding! Oh Jesus...I'm so sorry."

She pulled Irena to her feet, "Let's get you upstairs, cleaned up. I can't leave you in this state. Please, come on."

Irena stood up and allowed Tate to guide her upstairs. "That man is an animal."

"I just can't believe all this. I mean, was it Bill? Did he attack you?"

Irena turned and raised her eyebrows, "Do you really need me to answer that?"

"I've been stupid... the other woman, that's one thing...but attacking you...that...I just can't, I mean that makes him as bad as those low life who hurt me..."

177

"Finally, she sees the light. Now, enough about Bill. I'm sick of it. I warned you not to trust him."

Tate opened the bathroom cabinet, took out a handful of cotton wool and poured out a bowl of cooled boiled water from the kettle, "Here sit here." She gently pushed her friend into the chair and rested the bowl on the table. "I will be as gentle as I can be, okay." She dabbed at the raw skin on the back of Irena's head. It was because of her, Irena's attack; all because she refused to listen.

Irena grabbed her wrist and looked deep into her eyes, "Is it true?"

Tate flushed red, as she understood what Irena was asking, of course Bill had told her…and he would have loved doing so. Tate pulled her hands from Irena's grip and continued to dab away the dried blood. She said nothing, but her head nodded.

"Jesus Christ. I am lost for words. I am actually lost for fucking words."

Silence.

"WHAT THE FUCK WERE YOU THINKING TATE? HOW DID YOU JUSTIFY THAT DECISION? WHAT IF YOU GOT CAUGHT? WHAT IF YOU HAD GOT MURDERED OR RAPED?" Irena stood up and shook Tate's shoulders, the bowl of water smashed to the ground and water-soaked

Tate's feet. Tate sank to the floor and began to clear up the mess.

"Just leave it! For fucks sake Tate! It doesn't matter. LEAVE IT!" Irena's words pierced the air and Tate sat back on her heels and stared. She had never seen Irena lose control like that and it was all her fault. Her hands flew to her face and covered her shame.

"Why Tate? I thought we were doing okay? What made you agree to do something as stupid as smuggling drugs around?"

Tate rocked back and forth on her knees. Her sobs smothered any words she might have said.

"Please? I want to understand?" Irena whispered and knelt beside her. She pulled her hands away from her face and held onto them tightly.

Tate sniffed. "I'm so sorry, for everything. You gave me a home, when I had nowhere to go...you put me back together when I felt broken and supported me despite me not listening to you. But Paul brought Bills daughter over and threatened to make her do it...she's just a child really. I would never have forgiven myself..."

"And Bill would have been eternally grateful, eh?" Irena's head shook and she winced.

"You must be in so much pain...let me at least get you some pain killers?"

"I've had some. It'll be fine…Well ironically, I guess we have Tony to thank, his timing was impeccable. Just another 24 hours and you would have been up to your neck in it…Tate, you have to leave…"

"Bill won't be back here…he'll have bigger fish to fry and besides, I have enough money to catch whatever flight I want and I'm not leaving until I know you are ok."

"I'll only be ok, when you leave…please Tate?"

"First, before I go anywhere, I have a phone call to make."

Bill

Bill's car smashed into the lamp post outside an eerily silent Caminos. It was midnight and he seemed to have lost hours somewhere. A hazy recollection of some seedy little bar and a scrap with a local lurked. He should have gone straight to Caminos as planned. But thoughts of one last hurrah and a final piece of skirt lured him away. Now he was ready. His bloodied nose was clotting, and he was not sure if it was the onset of a hangover or the punch to the face, which caused his head to ache. He flicked a cigarette from the packet, and it fell to the floor as he clambered out. He reached to pick it up and staggered towards the bar. He pushed the door. It was locked. When was Caminos ever shut? Jose was always there.

"Open up. Let me in!" He screamed, pounding the doors with his bloodied fists but there was no response. He lifted his foot to kick them in and his grounded foot slipped from under him. As he fell backwards a shadowy figure, inside, caught his eye, his head struck the pavement and he blacked out.

SMOKE FILLED his nostrils, he was not sure if his eyes were open or closed, but he knew the smell of petrol. His car, perhaps he had crashed his car. He tried to move, but he felt bound, maybe he had become paralysed. He tried to focus his eyes, but it was too dark. He moved his head from side to side as footsteps approached. He would be rescued after all.

"I'm here. Please can you help me...I think I've crashed my car?"

No one answered. He strained to hear the footsteps, which sounded muffled but close by, maybe even circling him. Then he heard moans, they were on his level, near the ground...had he been driving with someone in the car? "Who's there?"

Then, a blinding light went on and he squinted. His eyes adjusted and he realised where he was. He was in the stock room of Caminos, and he was not alone. Paul lay gagged and bound in the corner by the empty crates. His face bloodied and his eyes swollen. Bill looked down the length of his own outstretched body now tied at the ankles and wrists. Confusion muddied the little coherency he held onto, if Paul was over there, then who was doing this.

His head flicked from one side to the other and cold sweat surged from his pores, as he scanned the room. He could see no one. Perhaps it was Tony come to finish them off. He tilted his head as far back as it would go, and there, towering behind him, was Jose.

Jose strode round to where Bills bound feet struggled and smiled, "Whiskey and ginger?"

"Jose?"

"It's a shame in a way that you have woken up. I thought I might have executed this next part without any awkward conversations. I knew I should have gagged you as well."

Bill's hazy mind suddenly cleared, and the taste of petrol clung to his throat. "Jose, you and me go back a long way...didn't I always do right by you?"

Jose smiled and nodded. "Oh yes, if throwing me the odd large tip is 'doing right'. You were lining up young women for drug runners...from this bar! Your own daughter Bill, how could you stoop so low? Everyone in this neighbourhood has had enough of your shit. You bring it to our door. I have witnesses to say they saw you two fighting. Your car is parked smashed up out the front; of course, I could never have done that part, so I thank you for your added evidence." Jose smiled and gave a shallow nod of appreciation.

"Jose, let me go. You and I – we can make a good team…"

Jose crouched down and lowered his voice, "Save it Bill…I'm not one of your women who hangs on your every word. I stood behind that bar for long enough to see how you operate. The way you all treat your women, walk around our town as if you own it…making demands and threats…"

"Jose, this is your livelihood… this bar is your life?"

"This bar has brought me misery. I have lost years of my family, being at the disposal of you all, for too long. The two of you will perish tonight but I bet the rest of them scurry away within twenty-four hours. As for this bar, it needs to burn. To purge the town of the wrong doings committed and planned within these walls."

Panic constricted Bill's voice to a hoarse mutter, "But Jose you need to support your family…please!"

"Oh, how generous of you Bill…thinking only of my poor family. Well, you see, I shall be well cared for, a young woman we both know has just come into some money! Fancy that! Lovely young woman, not had a great few years. Anyway, she has agreed to help me set up a new bar, one for families and decent people. You see, as you would put it, I have 'grown a pair' – finally."

Jose stood and took a box of matches from his pocket.

"They will know it's you – you won't get away with it...you'll go to prison and then what will your family do?"

"You know, in all these years none of you have told me to take a day off and spend time with my family, and now you are so concerned. Really, it's touching Bill. But you see, the Police are just as keen for this to happen and as we have witnesses..."

Bill fought against the binding, which cut into his skin. His ankles, also tied to the shelving, rocked them precariously as he jerked. This was his end, his hell. He turned to see Jose climb out of the window, into the courtyard, empty except for the old bike.

His wide eyes slowed every movement as Jose struck the match and flicked it into the stock room. Bill realised the screams he could hear were his own. Jose stood, watched to make sure the fire burned, jumped over the wall and away from the bar.

Bill's body writhed and fought to escape. His lungs coughed and choked with the rising smoke. As the shelving crashed down his final thought was of the person to blame for his demise, Tate.

Tate

Tate sat in the glossy first-class lounge at the airport and sipped a cold flute of champagne. She admired her freshly manicured nails and sighed. Saying goodbye to Irena had been tough, but she knew that she would go back once everything had settled back down. The visit back home to the UK, was purely an extended holiday. Irena and Maria had saved her, in so many ways and she would repay them somehow. She would show them the real Tate. Perhaps she would go on that date with Mauricio too, one day. However, now she understood why Irena operated in her way and realised that her happiness should begin with herself, not be reliant on any man. She would never give that power to another.

Jose's words of thanks comforted her. She was able to give him enough money to make up for all the crap Bill's lot had caused. Jose was discreet. He had to be working that bar. After the brutality of her beatings, he would carry her upstairs to his private room and gently patch her up, enough to get her home. He never judged her, in fact, his eyes were filled with pity, and he often advised her to leave. She shuddered. She needed to put those days behind her now. The newspapers were strangely silent about the messy end of Caminos. The second page contained a small article about the fire that destroyed the bar, stating the cause was due to tired electrical cabling.

No fatalities were reported or plans to rebuild; it was all swept neatly under the carpet.

Tate gazed at the mother and daughter who were settling on a nearby table. Her blood ran cold as she recognised them. She was the woman from the photographs, with Bill. Her head swam, who was she really? Did she know Bill? Was she his secret lover? Was the little girl Bills maybe? She stood and gathered her things, and before she could decide how to proceed, she was standing at their table, "Hi, mind if I join you? We met at the shop...when you bought the little dog. Back in Campo?"

"Oh Hi! Yes, I remember, small world it seems. Please sit," the woman spoke as she continued to put little pink headphones on her daughter, who was sleepy and wanted to watch a film. She pecked a kiss on her head and then sipped on her coffee, her narrow eyes fixed on Tate.

"So, did you have a good holiday?" Tate tried to keep it breezy.

"It was a lovely break away, thank you. You flying back to Gatwick too?"

"Uh huh." Silence followed and Tate shifted in her seat, "Tate, and you are?"

"Celia and this is Keira, my daughter."

"Where were you staying? Anywhere nice?"

"We stayed with a friend; I was helping out with some business whilst out here, so it worked well."

"Oh, I see. Look, I just want to know what went on with you and Bill."

Celia almost choked on her coffee at the mention of his name. Tate sensed her hesitation, but she wanted to know, so she could finally put him to rest, "Please, I know you owe me nothing, you don't even know me, but this really does mean a lot to me." Her sad eyes pleaded her cause.

Celia leaned in close after looking suspiciously around, "He was nothing to me. I was paid to spend time with him, lead him on. That is all. Nothing real happened between us. This whole first-class travel – all part of the deal. Keira and I no longer frequent the high life."

Tate needed a cigarette. It was all a set up. "So, you and he, I mean, you weren't lovers? She, I mean Keira is not his?"

Celia threw back her head with laughter, "Good God no! I never met him before this trip, and if I wasn't so short on cash, I would never have got involved. You are best off away from him, from what I saw, thinks his supposed charm works on everyone."

"Shit. I never saw that coming. I mean I knew the photographs were a set up, but you- a honey trap."

"Never did like that description," she winced. "I don't know why I'm telling you any of this, but there we go… Listen, I was told, on good authority, that Bill played a hand in my husband's sudden death. He was no angel, I'm under no illusion about that, but he didn't deserve to die. So, when this chance came up, to pay me to come out here, have a holiday and get a substantial payment to revenge his death, I couldn't say no. I don't know what the reasons were, nor do I wish to know any outcomes, but I know I feel as though I took back control, and got one up on him."

Tate downed her champagne, "Excuse me, two more champagnes please," she called to the waiter. "Well, Celia, you have guts, I'll give you that. It could have turned nasty for you, you know."

"I learned from a young age how to take care of myself, besides, you should see the size of my friend I stayed with, no one would mess with him!" She smirked. "Now Keira and I have money to live on, for a while anyway. Put it this way, my husband had no life insurance.

Tate shook her head and any last feelings harboured towards Bill, were quickly dissipating. The reality of her miraculous escape suddenly hit her and finally she could see a future without him. We all have a past, even Celia. She hoped to learn more about her one day. "Celia? Could I contact you at some point, I have plans, ideas and someone like you could make a great associate."

"Sure, here," she scrawled down her details onto a napkin and handed it to Tate, "this money won't last forever, and I have never been one for a nine to five, somehow, I sense that's not what you had in mind either?"

"Hmm. All in good time, but for now let's raise a toast: To Bill, for giving us this fresh start. No, not to Bill, to US, for taking the heat and putting things right."

I hope you enjoyed this story, and if you are interested in reading more, BOOK TWO – DEEPER STILL, is now available:

Tate is young, beautiful and successful. Her past is firmly behind her, and her eyes fixed on the future. Her shadowy past may have funded her lifestyle, but she deserved every penny, for what she suffered, right?

Ellie is determined to get her hands on everything her dad, Bill, had stolen from him whilst he perished in the fire. It is rightfully hers after all. But she is plagued by demons, and her drug habit feeds her darkness. Her arrival will shake Tate's new life to the core.

This story will sweep you up into the eye of a storm, as you watch the events unfold from both perspectives. Will anyone survive, as they fall DEEPER STILL.**?**

Writing is certainly a labour of love. The ideas, story development and then edit after edit is an extremely long process. Since my recent ME & FND diagnosis, I am a little slower at writing, so please bear with me!

If you have enjoyed this story, please do review it. I thank you in advance for your support in this, and please don't be shy with spreading the word about Tate and Bill...

Cover photo credit: Alex Perez
https://unsplash.com/photos/4AtyEKK36DI?utm_source=unsplash&utm_medium=referral&utm_content=creditShareLink

This is a work of fiction, as are the characters and situations.